A Cold Wind from the Andes

Selected Reviews

The Last Pope

"A truly great novel. I plan to make it my finest motion picture."
>—Martin Poll, producer of *The Lion in Winter*, starring Peter O'Toole and Katharine Hepburn

"A thrilling blend of history, religion, and human relationships."
>—*The New York Post*

"Packs a powerful punch … reminiscent of the Shoes of the Fisherman …"
>—Booklist

The Glass Tower

"Breathless introduction to the inner workings of big business …"
>—*The Times* Literary Supplement

"A vivid, fast moving story about people in PR."
>—*SHE* magazine

"[An] institution story perfected by Zola and none the worse for it … deftly, excitingly told."
>—*The Daily Telegraph*

"A sharp and entertaining first from Mr. Osborn, who is already an accomplished screenwriter."
>—*Lincolnshire Evening Telegraph*

Murder on Martha's Vineyard

"A good tale of mystery and murder. Its plot twists and turns in and out of an intriguing whodunit that packs a punch at the end powerful enough to floor one."
—*Western Morning News*

"This well-plotted thriller makes compulsive holiday reading."
—*Salisbury Journal*

"This is the first entry in what might become a promising new series.… Osborn has created an interesting protagonist."
—*Publishers Weekly*

"Before settling down to read this book, take the phone off the hook, make sure all the doors and windows are locked, set a large medicinal brandy within easy reach, and prepare to let David Osborn scare your pants off. Highly recommended."
—*The Bloodhound*

"Delightful mystery is a zinger. Every one of its 258 pages says 'turn me.'"
—*Chattanooga New Free Press*

Murder on the Chesapeake

"Satisfying tale … intrepid sleuth."
—*Publishers Weekly*

"The tale is spun tightly and the main characters are engaging."
—*Chicago Sun Times*

Open Season

"A truly brilliant novel … an accomplished writer in all media, but ultimately a pro … a superbly organized book, brutal, chilling, but carrying a terrible conviction."
    —*Canberra Times*

"As commercial and exciting a novel as can be found today.… It is shocking, savage, and graphic, a cruel book that spares little in detail. There is unbearable suspense, headlong action, and ends with a final ironic twist that will leave the reader gasping. Osborn is a master storyteller and his remorseless style matches his remorseless narrative.…"
    —*Abilene Reporter News*

"This well-plotted thriller makes compulsive holiday reading."
    —*Salisbury Journal*

"This is the first entry in what might become a promising new series.… Osborn has created an interesting protagonist."
    —*Publishers Weekly*

"Before settling down to read this book, take the phone off the hook, make sure all the doors and windows are locked, set a large medicinal brandy within easy reach, and prepare to let David Osborn scare your pants off. Highly recommended."
    —*The Bloodhound*

"Delightful mystery is a zinger. Every one of its 258 pages says 'turn me.'"
    —*Chattanooga New Free Press*

Murder on the Chesapeake

"Satisfying tale ... intrepid sleuth."
—*Publishers Weekly*

"The tale is spun tightly and the main characters are engaging."
—*Chicago Sun Times*

Open Season

"A truly brilliant novel ... an accomplished writer in all media, but ultimately a pro ... a superbly organized book, brutal, chilling, but carrying a terrible conviction."
—*Canberra Times*

"As commercial and exciting a novel as can be found today.... It is shocking, savage, and graphic, a cruel book that spares little in detail. There is unbearable suspense, headlong action, and ends with a final ironic twist that will leave the reader gasping. Osborn is a master storyteller and his remorseless style matches his remorseless narrative...."
—*Abilene Reporter News*

"David Osborn's story motif in *Open Season* is not new—the human set free to become the hunted, the quarry in a hunt made more exciting by the element of human intelligence and cunning on both sides. But Osborn who knows his way with a story and people and how to keep the suspense and relish boiling, gives it added spice and terror ... one of the season's top novels."
—*Waco* (Texas) *Tribune-Herald*

The French Decision

"Osborn's novel shrivels the nerves ... a gripping story skillfully developed ... the ironic epilogue [is] even more explosive."
    —*Publishers Weekly*

"An exciting, highly plausible Washington thriller ..."
    —Gore Vidal

"In a powerful story of industrial espionage which takes place in the United States and France, David Osborn examines American politics, the French economy, international high finance, and the Common Market as well as torture and love. He does it all with a gentle irony and without ever losing his perspective by deeply involving us in the troubled emotions of his hero, a young Arab posing as a Jew who takes American nationality to become a 'mole' in the service of French espionage...."
    —*L'Express*, Paris

"An unforgettable thriller of high-level intrigue ... this fictional world, vividly portrayed, is just realistic enough to be disturbing and unsettling.... Aaron Zeismann a real, brilliantly conceived character ... the climax of this flawlessly plotted story is stunning, as is its ironic epilogue. Anyone will find this thriller impossible to put down...."
    —*Pittsburgh Press*

"No better example of absorbing, fast-paced intrigue. Compelling to the last punctuation mark."
    —Clive Cussler

"Grisly serving of double-agenting and cat and mouse chases ... effective and understated ..."
    —*The Kirkus Review*

"fast-moving and hard to put down ..."
    —Associated Press

Love and Treason

"Spellbinding ... unbearable suspense ... compulsive reading ... what makes this novel even more than a thriller is the humanity of the characters...."
    —*The Pittsburgh Press*

"This is a first-class book. It has what one admires so often in English thrillers and finds so seldom in American ones: literate, accomplished writing which makes the plot more ingenious, the characterizations more deft and engaging, and therefore the thrills more thrilling...."
    —Michael Thomas, author of *Green Monday*

"There won't be a better book published in America this year.... brilliantly plotted ... infinite complications ... as audacious as it is original ..."
    —Alastair Maclean

"Taut and tender political thriller ... succeeds both as a thriller and a love story ..."
    —*Delta Air Lines* magazine

"Osborn captures the reader's interest almost at once and doesn't let it go."
    —*The Knoxville News-Sentinel*

A Cold Wind *from the* Andes

a novel by

David Osborn

DAGMAR MIURA

LOS ANGELES

Published by Dagmar Miura
Los Angeles
www.dagmarmiura.com

A Cold Wind from the Andes

First published 2017

ISBN: 978-1-942267-27-0

for Robin, with love

ONE

———◆———

Many if not most people live in a state of self-delusion, sincerely believing they are someone they are not and hiding, even from themselves, the real person they actually are. This was the thought of David Hahn as he settled comfortably into the soft leather surroundings of his chair and waited for the AD floor manager, standing between the two cameras in the TV studio, to signal that they were on the air. As the makeup woman gave a last hurried touch of powder to his seventy-year-old face, sensitively seamed with his weary knowledge of life, and ran a fast comb through his still heavily thick gray hair, he suspected it to be particularly true of the woman he was about to interview and who was seated in an equally comfortable chair directly across a low table between them that was stacked with a number of the best-selling books she'd authored.

Presuming her authoritative and confident demeanor, aided by her expensive Paris designer clothing and the short styling of her artificially platinum hair, was indicative of the real woman would be a mistake, he thought. Kelly Anders, only just forty and with looks and charm to match her success, was neither the woman the world presumed it knew nor the woman, he was equally certain, who, in all sincerity, she *thought* she was herself. With Kelly, years of experience told him, false self-perception hid reality just the way the intimacy of the corner scenery of the studio enveloped around them did. Its softly muted lighting, the lines of old books dignifying the floor-to-ceiling bookcase, the bowl of early-summer flowers, phlox and gladiolas in a niche below a faintly seen copy of a French Impressionist, all hid the functional reality of the studio beyond: the cameras, the lights, the shirt-sleeved cameramen, the young AD floor manager with his clipboard and his earphones whose youth seemed surreal. And behind all that, the opaque glass face of the control room where, seated before a bank of monitors, the director, along with the producer, the production secretary, and the rep from the advertising agency, watched the long red second hand of a wall clock match the digital on his monitor as it pulsed one second after another, irrevocably upward toward the number 12.

Until, on David Hahn's laptop, unobtrusively nestled in his lap, there was the sudden appearance of the show's logo, *Face to Face—Live, with David Hahn.*

It shared a split-screen listing of his more important notes—background on the woman he was to interview, questions to ask her. And in his earpiece, there was the studio voice of the announcer, geared to suggest an almost reverent dignity in the program.

David looked away from the laptop, heard the director's voice count down, "five, four, three, two, one … It's all yours, David," saw the jerked hand-signal from the floor manager, and he was on the air, the red light of one of the cameras winking on simultaneously as the camera faced close in on him.

"Good evening. I'm David Hahn, and tonight my guest is a woman known to millions for her authorship of one outstanding novel after another that have given her an almost unchallenged position for the past three years at the top of the *New York Times* best-seller list. Please join me in welcoming Kelly Anders to *Face to Face*."

She straightened, crossing one slender leg over the other, her jeweled hand flashing light as she adjusted her tailored skirt and with an animated smile favored him in a soft, slightly husky voice. "Thank you, David. It's wonderful to be with you."

Hahn then went to work in the relaxed and disarming way that had made his Sunday-night prime-time show shatter Nielsen records. Pre-broadcast, he had briefed her on the questions he would ask, and she'd only had one request. It was not to overly dwell on her husband and the terrible incident three years previous that had left him a virtual vegetable.

A management consultant with a continued brilliant career in front of him, Gerald Evarts had gone with the board chairman and president of Eurocon, a European parent corporation that owned a gold mining company in Argentina, to check out what was becoming a losing operation. Along with a photographer and the young woman companion of the chairman with whom he had apparently become intimate, Gerald was kidnapped by a small group of dissident miners and held captive for ransoming in the mountainous foothills of the towering Andes. After the young woman was terribly injured attempting an escape that failed and Gerald himself had been beaten nearly to death in a subsequent successful attempt, he had survived only when the photographer managed to free both of them.

"Regardless of the scandal, I don't think, and I don't want people to think," she'd said quietly when they'd first met and discussed the program, "that I am any saint for sticking with Gerald and taking care of him. I loved him and, like any other person, he does not deserve love to stop simply because he is unable to respond."

He'd been impressed by that and impressed, too, as he almost always was with authors, with an aura about her of confident, no-nonsense professionalism. This came, he knew, from lonely years at a computer making the endless hard choices that were hers and nobody else's to make. Authoring a novel was a long and difficult process and required as much skilled craftsmanship as intuitive inspiration or the indefinable uniqueness of raw talent.

Now, with his usual fatherly graciousness that had made him almost a household icon, he steered her through routine questions about her beginnings, the early years viewers were always curious about where any celebrity was concerned.

"You were born and raised in Chicago."

"In a suburb, yes. Lincoln Park."

"Your father was in business?"

"Yes, he ran a small company that manufactured kitchen utensils."

"Not typewriters."

Laughter. "No."

"And, sadly you lost him when very young."

"I was ten, yes."

"And then, quite soon after, you lost your mother."

"Yes. She wasn't very well and didn't last a year. Basically I was raised by an aunt, my mother's sister."

"And lost her, too, I understand."

"When I was in college, yes. She was a wonderful woman, divorced for many years. I never saw her husband. I was very fond of her."

"And that left you on your own. You were how old?"

"Twenty."

"But you managed."

She laughed lightly. "Yes. It wasn't easy, but you can't simply cave in and stop because others have. You keep going."

"And in your case, to brilliant success and a stellar marriage."

"Well, I don't know how brilliant, but yes. And my husband's a wonderful guy."

So much for the lie, Hahn thought, a well-guarded but relatively minor one in comparison to the self-delusion with which she almost certainly hid from herself the person she really was. He was relieved to get it over with and out of the way just the same, even as he vaguely wondered why she clung to it. Did she fear the truth would somehow reduce the picture-perfect image of a top-of-the-line author, married to a successful business executive with a Mayflower background, one whose family had apparently suppressed worries due to her literary success over the relative obscurity of her background? Or was she simply driven by such ambition that she felt her background an anchor? If so, that flew against the popularity always given to the notion of rags-to-riches and didn't seem at all like the woman he was interviewing.

Fact: her name originally was neither Kelly nor Anders. She was born Kaja Arzejwski and Polish. She'd had her name legally changed either in college or slightly before. Her parents had never been found; Arzejwski was not an uncommon name and there was possible evidence that her father might have been a butcher working in one of Chicago's slaughterhouses. There had never been an aunt, alive or deceased. Kelly had been placed by social welfare organizations in a number of foster homes, both private and official, that were located not in any relatively gentrified sub-urb like Lincoln Park but in one of the tougher South Side Chicago neighborhoods where air pollution and smog choked out lives long before their natural time, and families lived in shabby and often unheated rooms with gunshots punctuating uneasy nights as teen gangs fought it out, heedless of whom they destroyed.

He'd been curious, too, when he'd learned it, as to exactly when she'd decided to abandon all that and assume the new life. And why? The researcher, who'd unearthed the information only after extensive work, hadn't been able to uncover any school records under her original name, nor the name of her aunt. Back when he had been a network reporter, David knew he would have gone for it and exposed her. But he wasn't that young man any longer, and *Face to Face* wasn't a pro-gram selling sensationalism. If there was to be a "dis-covery" and fodder for the tabloid press, he didn't want *Face to Face* connected with it. He'd told his researcher to lay off and bury the information.

Besides, he had decided, all of that was basically irrelevant. Of far greater interest and perhaps concern was who the Kelly was that her self-delusion denied? He felt there was a link where her writing was con-cerned. Disclosed, it might force her to face a complete stranger in herself, which could possibly be disturb-ing or even painful to her. That was an area he would also avoid. Digging too deep could ruin an interview. It would remain, if ever, for some future interviewer or event to produce revelation. Meanwhile he was stuck with his inherent curiosity. Let it suffice that she supposedly came from a middle-class American background, had married a successful businessman from a Mayflower family, and had soared high as an author in her own right.

He continued with his time-proven interview formula. "Kelly, the thing everyone would like to know about you, I'm sure, is when you started to write. Not just when, but more importantly, *why*."

She seemed thoughtful a moment and then said, "David, I'm not really sure. I think my last year in college. I only went to a community college near Lincoln Park, and I took a writing course because basically I was a lousy student and I thought it would be easy. To my surprise I found it *was* easy. I mean the essays the instructor ordered up. He was a really nice guy and urged me to read the classics and gave me a long list of them, which I did, and somewhere along the line I knew I'd fallen on what I could productively do to earn a living in life: write novels."

That rang true to him, and he went on with questions that were fairly common knowledge. "And your first one was a disaster?"

"Worse. And not just the first one. I think the second was just as bad. I sent them to endless lists of publishers, and most of the time never got a reply."

"But one day you did. Novel number three."

Laughter. "Number four, actually. Number three—well, only half of a novel really—ended up in the furnace like one and two."

"And since then, when you hit on a successful formula aimed at women, you've turned out fifteen more, and all saw print. That's quite a body of work in a relatively few years."

"Fortunately I write pretty fast, and I don't really think of it as work, David, although I suppose it is. Once I get a story going, it takes on a life of its own that is somehow separate from me. I mean, like most writers, I lead a double life and all that. I'm really quite a schizophrenic."

"Do you have a regular routine … specific hours? I know most writers do."

"Oh, yes. I'm almost drearily nine-to-five where actually putting things down on paper is concerned. Well, more honestly ten-to-four. I can't keep things going much longer than that. If I do, what I write starts not to make sense. Otherwise, I write all the time—in my head, I mean. When I do a book, it becomes my life twenty-four hours a day."

"And now the big question, Kelly. Your novels for the most part are aimed at women and concerned with a drive in some to find self-expression, even assertive self-confidence, to not mold to the conventions of society and what is too often expected of them. In a way to be themselves, the inner them, and not the outer woman much of the world still unfortunately requires. Is that a fair appraisal?"

This led her in a discussion of several of her more famous books and went on from there: What gave her an idea for one?—*Probably someone she met or some incident or other.* How much of her thinking was geared to what would sell best?—*Quite a bit. Like everyone she needed to make a living.* Why she only wrote about women?—*Perhaps because she saw men more in a sexual way. She wrote about souls, not sex, and women were the more romantic and familiar gender.*

"And since women read far more than men and so were a larger market for your product?"

"Exactly."

While seemingly simple, her answers gave her the chance to elaborate, and he was pleased that she took over the interview in a way that minimized him. It was what he and his producer wanted *Face to Face* always to do. As the interviewer, he should be only an instrument that brought out the person being interviewed.

As she'd requested, he went easy on the Argentinian disaster, but David wondered how the incident affected her writing since. What part did the rumored affair her husband had had there play in the assertive attitudes of the women she more recently wrote about? By the time the interview was over and there was the usual post-show, bright-light bustle around him and her, dispelling all sense of intimacy, he realized he'd been fascinated by her and wished he hadn't been so restrained. There were moments when, in spite of her confident polish, he had detected an odd vulnerability, a hint of someone who beneath it all felt lost, and when she left the studio he felt he'd gained but little insight into the real woman he was certain Kelly so successfully

hid even from herself. For him she remained an unresolved and complex enigma.

TWO

When Kelly left the TV studio she saw she'd spent too much time saying good bye to everyone. And then as she left the building at a darkened studio side door where a courtesy limo waited, she was taken aback by a small cluster of admirers wanting her autograph or a book signed. She generally didn't like signing books. She hated the pushiness of so many of her readers who seemed to think she was obliged to write her name in books for them whether she cared to or not. But tonight was slightly different. Hahn had been penetrating, and, rather to her surprise, she had felt vaguely insecure throughout the interview, and still did. Her exiting the side door of the TV studio and facing fans gave her an unexpected lift. She had a sudden sense of theatre, the slightly glamorous feeling of being an actress fresh from a stage success, and for a short while she found herself actually enjoying the awe and reverence for the untouchable magician who had brought escape into the often dreary lives that lay within the circle of eager faces spontaneously pressing in around her.

It was rush hour, a time in New York when everything that moves comes to a virtual halt: the heavy flow of traffic in a cacophony of sound that was like a dark river of barely moving sludge between banks of oppressively towering buildings, and people a knotted, immovable swarm of crushed-together, desperate bodies for the moment mindless of anything else—humanity become anonymous nonentities at every intersection.

It was twenty minutes before Kelly could get away and nearly another forty minutes in the limo's overheated interior that smelled faintly of someone else's perfume before the driver, endlessly complaining in unintelligible English—Serbian, Albanian, Russian?—dropped her off on Manhattan's lower west side at the tall new residential building that was home. Flanking a gentrified brownstone tenement and market district, it looked out over the busy West Side Highway and beyond to where ships once docked and where now a mile-long recreational area of bicycle and pedestrian paths bordered the Hudson River in a virtual avenue of green trees. When Gerald had returned from Argentina she had moved there from a hugely spacious loft apartment in a still cobbled street of Tribeca. It was in a six-story warehouse that once housed olives and spices, the exotic odor of which still lurked in every aspect of its structure, and during her tenancy, it had also been occupied by two well-known film stars, a celebrated designer of women's sports clothes, and a famed illustrator and cartoonist.

She'd loved the place, but the new building, with every possible modern convenience and twenty-four-hour doormen, had seemed a better place for Gerald. The rent on the four-bedroom penthouse, occupying half of an entire floor, was exorbitant but was worth it. Gerald was able to have his own small suite: his bedroom, a bath and a sitting room for his nursing staff who came and went, one at a time, in shifts of eight hours. She paid them courtesy of the insurance settlement she'd extracted in endless legal action from Eurocon's Argoronorte, the Argentinian gold mining company that had been Gerald's client.

In her own spacious bedroom, a short distance away, she'd spared nothing. It was deep-carpeted with a king-size bed and a walk-in closet. Her bathroom was marble tiled and heavily mirrored with both a tub, if she felt in the mood to soak, and a glass-walled walk-in shower for daily use. In a dressing alcove there was an eighteenth-century French provincial dressing table or *poudreuse*. She had hung well-lit framed prints of French impressionists on fabric walls, and sliding glass doors opened onto a part of the wide terrace that wrapped around building.

A much smaller room at the apartment's far end and intended for a maid served as her work room, and was sparsely furnished with only a wide, flat desk occupied by her PC as well as her laptop. Next to it, a file case and some bookshelves were both topped by potted plants. Close by was the room and bath of Estella, her permanent housekeeper, a short and rotund middle-aged Latina, originally from Nicaragua, who had become indispensable to her.

Getting out of the smoothly modern elevator into the silent foyer she shared with the other penthouse tenant, the owner of a major art gallery, and where there was subdued wallpaper and a big bowl of artificial flowers on a side table, she was greeted by the muffled barking of Mischief. The solidly chunky pit bull–like mutt she'd adopted two years previous was always aware of some faint vibration of sound, apparent only to her, that would announce long before they arrived that someone was coming up on the elevator. Kelly was still fishing about in her shoulder bag for her keys when her door abruptly opened, and she found herself looking at Estella's warmly smiling face.

"Oh, hi, Estella. Mischief, calm down. Good girl."

Estella got hold of the frantically happy dog by the collar and laughed. "I think she must have heard you getting out of the limo. I watched you on TV along with Mr. Townsend. Kelly, you were just wonderful."

Kelly gave her a quick hug and then said, "I doubt I was, but thank you just the same. Is Mr. Townsend here, then?" There was surprise in her tone.

"Him and Mr. McKain."

"Arson? Oh, my God, I'd completely forgotten." Kelly cursed inwardly. So much for a quiet drink, an early dinner, and then bed.

"You were expecting him?"

"I was originally supposed to meet him at his office, and I'd asked him to meet me here instead of going there because of the TV thing. He wants to discuss a book-signing tour of England." As Estella helped her slip out of her coat, Kelly glanced at her watch. "And look at the time. It's past seven."

"Bad traffic?"

"Every avenue was a parking lot, even down past fourteenth."

"Will you be eating out or in?"

"I think in, Estella. I'm too beat to cope with outside right now. Maybe you could order up some sandwiches from the deli. I guess I'll have to offer to feed people."

"Not a problem."

Turning to go, Kelly hesitated. "Gerald?"

"As usual. The new nurse is good."

"Tell her I'll drop by later. And, Estella, tell the two gentlemen I'll be with them in a minute." Kelly flashed a silent smile at the older woman and went to her bedroom. She shed the suit she'd worn at the interview, put on a housecoat and checked her makeup, and then, taking a deep breath, she went on into the living room, where a designer decor of modern mixed with French provincial complimented a solid wall of glass, flanked by silk drapes that gave onto a flagstone terrace she'd had planted with shrubbery and with several ornamental trees rooted in enormous wooden tubs.

She'd objected to the trees but had been overridden

by her interior decorator. In their size, they hit close
to home in reminding her of the poor city-abused and
stunted little crab apple in a rubbish-cluttered empty
Chicago South Side lot of her childhood that was a
last sad remnant of a once small park. Sandwiched
forlornly between two towering buildings, the lot was
fenced, but often she had sneaked in anyway, crawling
through a ragged hole in the rusty wire to make a cau-
tious way through the towering weeds and ugly sumac
saplings that rose amongst scattered empty cans and
broken bottles. Reaching the tree, she'd touch it gently, sensing somehow the miracle of it being alive and
feeling a kinship to it. "Fairies live in it," she was told
by a kind-faced city worker who hadn't let the police
know that she'd ignored the "Entry Forbidden" sign
on the fence.

There was the tree, first all for herself and then
for Tonky, too, the little black kid with one withered
leg and her only true friend, who'd showed up one
day painfully shuffling along foot by foot, his bat-
tered and mismatched crutches barely held together
with tape. They'd made a garden together almost out
of sight against the wall of one of the tall buildings
framing the empty lot, replanting flowering weeds
and a packet of seeds Tonky had found fallen from
a garbage can someplace, bringing water scooped up
from gutters in cans after rains, and fresh dirt stolen
from city parks. The little tree and the garden was
their *safe place*, a refuge where Tonky wasn't pushed
aside because he was a cripple and black and laughed

at, and her because she wasn't wanted anywhere. No matter Tonky's pain or the severity of her often unheated two-room home and sometimes lack of food, the coarse and angry resentment at her presence; the little tree and the garden were always there for her and Tonky, living entities they could talk to and love.

Until one day they weren't. And in their place a monstrous backhoe, its treads crushing the garden into the rubble of brick and cement, hard-hatted men looking over unrolled blue prints, the poured-concrete and steel beginnings of an office building, a picture of it on the half-removed fence—a tall glittering glass tower. And on a big truck moving out debris, the little crab apple, pathetically broken and crushed.

The two men rose, drinks in hand as Kelly entered, Townsend, balding in his fifties, his rugby-player build complimenting his once fame as a top-seeded tennis player and a winner at Wimbledon, the slight redness of his skin, the loosening of his jowls and beginnings of eye paunches betraying drink along with the faintly blue eyes themselves that seemed never to quite meet another's. Arson, slender, gray, closer to a slightly stooped seventy befitting his eminence as head of Crossroads Publishing's empire, for which he all too readily applauded himself. Light glinted from steel-rimmed spectacles set high above the bridge of his prominently long nose, and his British origins were betrayed the moment he spoke.

"There she is." He came forward, both arms outstretched, his thin lips smiling.

Kelly embraced him, then Townsend, but the younger man with a hint of reticence. "Hi, Phil. Surprise. I didn't expect to see you until tomorrow." That with also a vague hint of annoyance in her tone.

If he felt the slight rebuff he didn't show it. "I'd had enough Washington for a lifetime and had a chance at a flight." He emphasized Washington the same way he would always speak with false familiarity of those who were politically influential with "Been seeing friends on the Hill." Having done nothing since his tennis days, he boosted his image of self-importance at any chance, especially if he'd encountered a well-known celebrity or politician whom he would then, whenever possible, refer to by first name.

Kelly gave him a slightly askance look and turned back to McKain. "Arson, I'm so sorry to be so late."

"Nonsense. You were being seduced by that David Hahn fellow into selling another half million books. Clever bugger, that little man, the way he gets the best out of people. Got to hand him that. Found himself a gimmick that pays—other people's success. You were quite wonderful, dear girl. As usual, of course. And, oh! I haven't forgot your British book tour itinerary, incidentally. Don't forget to remind me to give you a copy before I leave."

"I won't, and you're not about to leave for a while,"

Kelly said firmly, pretending pleasure. She hated book tours and couldn't imagine why she had ever agreed to this one. Why on earth had she? Perhaps just the thought of London and the chance to get away for ten days? She didn't know. Something nagged. Some hidden reason? Not wanting to think of it any more, she collapsed on one of the couches. "Estella is ordering some sandwiches and we can all pick *Face to Face* to bits. Phil, you're going to have to listen to Arson and I talking business."

"Not a problem. I've got you on replay and I'll watch you again."

You can make us all drinks first. A margarita for me, thank you. Arson?"

"A vodka on the rocks would be splendid."

It was the beginning of an evening that started with Kelly feeling first worn out from her television interview, which had left her feeling unusually unsure of herself, and then the nervousness from the traffic that had kept her far too long from the safety of her apartment. It ended with her feeling thoroughly exhausted when close to midnight her publisher finally left. She'd quickly dismissed talk of the interview. Although to be on *Face to Face* was to reach the pinnacle of success, she'd long ago found that the true mark of it lay in modesty. Besides, she had really been uncomfortable every second of being televised. She'd liked David Hahn, he knew when to dig and when not to, she'd soon seen that, yet there'd always been the fear he might suddenly dig too far.

And talking about what she felt, what had moved her the most in which book she'd written when writing it, always confused and irritated her. She felt rarely moved, rarely emotional when writing. She constructed stories and made up people to go with them. It was carefully piling well-fitted brick onto brick. She didn't like to roll around in some sort of neurotic outpouring the way some authors did when talking about the beauty or hell of life, what it all meant. Or their blaming or praising fate and its inevitability or the lack of it—that and everything else they could drag out of the barrel to prove to themselves that they could think better and wiser than those who read their golden words. All right, she sneered, but so what. She rode high, sold books like the devil herself when others didn't.

After McKain's departure and when Estella said good night and went to her own little room that Kelly had had specially furnished and decorated for her, Kelly was unable to hide her irritation at Townsend still being there. To make things worse, he clearly expected to spend the night, rooting himself with yet another vodka in one of the deep chairs, feet up on the picture books on the glass cocktail table. His being her lover had long ago been accepted by Estella, who in her foreign worldliness saw nothing wrong in his breakfast appearances several times a week, barely covering his nakedness with a short terry cloth robe—women had lovers, men had mistresses, that's what made the world turn. But deep in her heart, Kelly knew she was beginning to tire of Townsend.

They had begun their relationship very soon after Gerald had returned on a stretcher from Argentina, mute, his body unmoving, his eyes staring fixedly at some point in space and seemingly unaware of any or anything around him. Townsend had been something of a balm at the deep wound she suffered when she'd learned through the glee of an unrestrained media of her husband's affair with the woman in Argentina. Why, why, why, when she and Gerald, she'd thought, had for over ten years been the perfect couple? At least that's what everyone said. Although some of their initial excitement over each other had dulled a little, wasn't that normal in any marriage?

Townsend had relieved some of the darkest moments—her first reaction of bewildered hurt and fighting with shock over Gerald's injuries, and then her inevitable anger. Feeling desperately insecure at a party one night, she'd got an unexpected lift from Townsend's aggressively coming on to her with clear bed intentions, and she'd soon found further refuge in the wild social life he led her into with all that peculiarly egocentric *in* crowd of New Yorkers who believed their people-choked, steel-and-concrete monolith was true earthly paradise. And there'd been more escape when they'd had sex—she'd never felt it love—when his muscular hard body seemed to follow him into her and fill her whole being with the excitement of the hungered male. And when she'd had her own moments in the subjugating triumph of her own ecstasy, there had always been the lingering bitterness and incomprehension about

Gerald. Why with another woman? Why?

"Kelly, why the hell do you keep him the way you do? He's a living goddamned corpse, for Christ's sake. Accept it. Get on with life. And while we're at it, how do you think I feel about having him there?" That was Townsend, waving angrily at Gerald's room down the hall. Jealous one night after too much vodka.

And Arson McKain. "Kelly, he's a bloody albatross around your neck. Get a lawyer, mine if you want, and relieve yourself of him: divorce, a nursing home, dump him back on his parents, whatever. Not a problem, I'm sure. You have every right."

She'd sometimes thought to but hadn't, and so Gerald lay there, a few rooms away, apparently unable to hear or speak and—the doctors said—probably didn't even think or know himself that he existed. What real reason than to keep him with her, silent and motionless, his pale face expressionless, the IV lines and the oxygen tubes in his nose mute companions. What reason to keep, a non-husband? Why not put him away in a home someplace. She didn't really know why, regardless of what she'd told David Hahn. For what had been? To flatter herself with benevolence? For a pristine public image—the widow who in spite of everything … "until death do us part … ?"

She had only been able to say what she's said to David Hahn—why she kept him—because she hadn't been able to think of any other explanation. It had come out of her involuntarily and as a surprise to herself. But what did it mean? She wasn't sure. And wasn't even sure she wanted to know. Gerald was there—the man who had once loved her, or said he did, the man she'd trustingly never doubted, lying silent and *unliving* in his room with a nurse, an anonymous being who kept him alive with the doctor's nightly medication that Townsend had once not so subtly suggested should be skipped one time and end it all.

On his way out Arson McKain's thoughts were on the projected book tour of England. And more, for what he hadn't told Kelly was what he'd added to it—a meeting, arranged through his London office, between her and Rachel Sommerset, the great British writer who was the previous year's winner of the Nobel prize for literature. Sommerset, reportedly something of a recluse and living in the countryside far out of London, had also won the coveted Man Booker award as well as the coveted French Prix Goncourt and was honored in South America by her lifelong friend and also Nobel prize winner, García Márquez. He was going to be able to use the meeting, McKain thought, to promote Kelly Anders, number one in Crossroads' stable of writers, to even greater sales success in the United States. He would link what he secretly considered Kelly's slick, for-women commercialism with true greatness. It was bound to be pure gold in even greater amounts than she was already earning for him. In spite of all that, Kelly would have balked at it, he knew; perhaps for all her success she'd feel compelled to avoid the great writer, although he couldn't imagine why. Could a truly great writer make her feel inferior, threaten her chic confidence in her own success? Whatever; he'd have to break it to her sooner or later. Perhaps once she was on the plane and over the Atlantic.

❖

Half an hour later, Phil Townsend took the same elevator downstairs to his Aston-Martin waiting in the building's subterranean parking lot. Kelly had said quietly and without anger, "Phil, forgive me, but not tonight. I'm desperately tired. I need to be alone. So please, just send me off to bed. Okay?" The thought of sex with him had suddenly revolted her. But cajoling had only made him more insistent. Until, almost shouting it, "Please, Phil. Please!" she left him to sulk by himself in the living room and in her bedroom had firmly locked the door behind her.

When she'd gone, Townsend helped himself to another drink and when later driving away felt a surge of anger that eclipsed the sexual ache in his loins. What the hell had got into Kelly? She was usually so receptive. Tired was nonsense. Kelly was *never* tired. Suspicion like a clenched fist suddenly came at him. Had she begun to find interest elsewhere? Jesus, fucking Christ, he wasn't going to tolerate that shit. He'd find out who it was, one way or another, and proceed from there. He'd never had trouble shouldering off any other man. Uptown and before he reached his own small apartment on the East Side, he stopped off at the Polo Bar. He needed another drink, and there were always attractive women there, waiting for whatever.

—➤ ◄—

In her dressing room and removing her makeup, Kelly knew she was finished with Phil Townsend. "Face it, Kelly," she thought, "he's become a bore," and she wondered how she'd ever had strong feelings about him. Shaking him out of her mind, she went to the bathroom, glad to be alone. She'd brushed her teeth and had put on a light cotton nightie when she thought again of David Hahn and the interview. He'd seemed a nice person and he'd stuck with his promise not to delve too deeply into Gerald's misfortune, or hers because of it. Then why had she felt insecure and strangely on the defensive with him. Thinking back, she felt the same way all over again. But why? What on earth was the matter with her? He hadn't asked a single question any different from those she'd had to answer in many another interview. Was it because there were moments when she felt Hahn, so intellectually superior to most, wasn't truly impressed by her as a writer nor care much for her best-selling works? If so, what writer *would* impress him? Probably none. Or had Hahn felt all during the interview that she wasn't being frank in her answers or thoughtful enough about her own works when actually she had been?

Or something else? Yes, something had lurked, there'd been something in his eyes when they'd talked before the interview. But what? She couldn't find any answers. Feeling unresolved—she hated it when things didn't fit or go smoothly—she got into bed, faintly hearing, as she did, the murmured voices of Estella and a nurse coming in from the elevator foyer. The shift was changing with the nurse coming on who would stay until eight in the morning and be responsible for Gerald's medication. Lying with her bedside light still on, she forced back vague guilt at not having looked in on him to say a ritual good-night as she always did before turning in. She would enter the little room, barren save for his special hospital bed and vital signs monitor with its winking red lights, to stare silently down at his motionless being, at his waxen, pale face with the oxygen tubes in his nostrils and the IV drip coming from the pole by the bed into one inert arm. It was always a moment when she didn't know what she felt, when she only experienced a kind of numbness in her heart. She would stand a few moments, looking at him, then murmur a whispered "Good night, Gerald," and after a few words with the nurse on duty, she would leave.

She knew she should do that now, get out of bed and go to his room. But she didn't. She forced the picture of him from her mind and tried instead to concentrate on the UK book signing schedule that Arson had left for her. Deep inside herself, she had a dull feeling that the only reasons she'd agreed to the English tour was to get away from Gerald and the life his condition from the ghastly happening in Argentina had forced on her. But after a while she turned out the bedside light and in the dark, letting all of today slip away into the silence, she began, as she so often did, to think about Tonky and their little garden and the stunted little crab apple tree standing forlornly and uncared for in the ugly rubble of the Chicago empty lot. What had happened to Tonky? Where had their little tree gone?

Thinking that way, she suddenly knew she was going to cry without knowing why and, in spite of herself, began to, until she told herself not to be silly, and made herself stop thinking about anything, and fell asleep.

THREE

◆

Three years earlier, when Lufthansa flight 955 was about six hours from Buenos Aires, Jake Barlow awoke and slowly took measure of where he was and why. The economy-class section of the big Airbus 330, flying through the night at thirty-five thousand feet above the Atlantic, was in semidarkness. Most of the passengers were asleep save for a few reading by the tubular shafts of light coming down from their seats' overhead lights. He felt mildly hungover from drinking too much when they'd taken off—first a stiff scotch, then several glasses of wine in hoping to disguise the stodgy German meal served up for dinner soon after they had left from Geneva on the long seventeen-hour haul across Spain and North Africa and then the south central Atlantic.

Hungover and miserably cramped, he'd been wedged too long in a seat that as every minute of the flight passed seemed more and more of an inescapable torture cell, one that was insistently overflowed into by the hugely overweight, balding German businessman in the seat next to him. He thought enviously of Gerald Evarts. He'd undoubtedly be stretched out ahead in one of the business-class seats that at night became so-called beds. He felt vaguely angry, too, at the first-class passengers flying in even greater luxury. Their privileged numbers included Alberto Castenelli, the board chairman of Eurocon, the European conglomerate that counted among its many acquisitions the Argentinian gold mining corporation, Argoronorte, of which he was titular president.

As a management consultant, Gerald was under contract to sort out what was causing Argoronorte to suffer a noticeable drop in profits. Jake, in turn hired to photograph every aspect of the Argentinian operation, including all Argentinian executives, had met Gerald at Eurocon headquarters in Geneva and had found him to be in his forties, well set up and exuding the kind of class confidence Jake had seen elsewhere in what he had always thought of as the Ivy League crowd. Cheerfully friendly but a little full of himself, Jake thought. He didn't hesitate to let Jake know he'd built his own sizeable firm from scratch and that he had none but blue-chip clients like Eurocon, an account he felt important enough to handle himself.

Alberto Castenelli was a different kettle of fish. He was a softly unathletic Italian nobleman and billionaire who wore immaculate Italian tailoring and faintly pungent men's perfume to match. He had platinum blond hair cropped so short that his rather narrow head with its small, slightly entrenched ears, long, thin nose, and weak chin looked almost shaven. He owed both his considerable wealth and a title, *count*, Gerald confided, to the fortune his ardently fascist father had garnered through corruption when in charge of an Italian African colony under Mussolini prior to World War Two. In the little Jake had seen of him so far—a brief, condescending handshake at the Geneva airport—Castenelli displayed all the arrogance one would expect from an excessively wealthy, nouveau riche title, Italian variety.

"You've been well recommended, Mr. Barlow. I hope you live up to it. I will want pictures of every aspect of the mine, even the offices. And certainly of all the executive personnel. There've been problems with the miners, I've been told. You'd think they'd be glad to have a job. The usual communists, probably. I'll want photos, too, of whoever are their leaders."

Jake said he would try to oblige while thinking that it had to be a cushy job compared to hiking a hundred miles into the Columbia jungle to photograph exotic birds for the *National Geographic*. That and ducking bombs in Syria as a free-lance way to pay rent for a year, as well as fighting off mosquitoes photographing boat people in Vietnam in order to pay for a divorce.

He wrestled himself out of his seat, went to the bathroom to relieve himself, and on the way back heard the first, softly muted notes of a guitar. Then, on reaching his seat, he began to hear voices singing a lilting gaucho melody and the muted conversation of people who had suddenly appeared like wraiths out of the semi-darkness of their various seats to stand about casually talking and laughing, some dancing to the guitar. One or two, who must have felt about the airline seats the same way he did, were uninhibitedly stretched out to sleep on the carpeted aisle and earning muttered disapproval from fellow German passengers who remained stiff and disapproving in their seats. A frantic hostess went rushing by shouting *"Achtung, Achtung"* and then, in hopeless frustration, *"Bitte! Bitte!"* Someone had lit a forbidden cigarette and its pungent odor had drifted up the aisle to her. There was more laughter and the guitar music became louder.

"If this is Argentina," Jake thought, "I like it," and hoped his time there would be as pleasantly uplifting in spite of whom he was with and what he was there for.

Getting his camera gear through customs at Buenos Aires when they landed turned out to be a sticky business, but it often was, no matter what country he visited, and over the years he'd visited nearly all one could. It proved to Jake that officialdom was basically hostile to journalists and especially to photographers. A kind of paranoia existed, he always noticed, that caused officialdom to see a camera, especially one with accompanying big zoom lenses, as there to spy out national secrets, or engage in some other antinational hostility. Or even conceal a bomb.

On arrival, Alberto Castenelli was immediately

whisked off by limousine to the five-star Four Seasons hotel along with his gnome-like personal valet, a poor little obsequious whipped dog called Gino. With him went the woman Jake supposed was Castenelli's secretary or possibly even his girlfriend. She was a surprisingly ordinary looking person in her mid-thirties with nondescript brown hair and a vaguely tired face who wore a fashionable designer suit and some expensive jewelry. Castenelli addressed her with ill-concealed chauvinism only as Teresa. Looking harried and vaguely embarrassed, she was clearly in charge of their baggage, tickets, and everything else that the Italian felt it beneath him to handle himself.

Left to their own devices, Jake and Gerald Evarts went by taxi to the Intercontinental with instructions for meeting their flight the next day in a corporate jet from Buenos Aires to Catamarca. The sprawling provincial city was on a wide semiarid plain in the far northwest where Argentina nudged Bolivia and was separated from Chile by the giant snow-capped Andes. It was an hour and a half away, and the flight to it would be over nearly six hundred miles of virtually uninhabited near desert. Jake was always to remember his surprise at how big and varied and underpopulated Argentina was, how different the wilderness of Patagonia, over two thousand miles to the south with its mountains and rushing streams, from the high-altitude semiarid plains and badlands of the far north, with, in between, the lush green of the endlessly flat Pampas with its huge herds of beef.

At Catamarca they would pick up two mining engineers and some office equipment for a second quick flight of thirty minutes to Fiambala. This was an isolated frontier town of twenty-five hundred and a hot springs tourist spa and jumping off point for hiking and cycling through the rugged Andean foothills that lay just to the west. There they would spend the night before driving on rough dirt roads some forty-odd miles farther up a tortured narrow valley to the actual Argoronorte mining site.

With most of a day and an evening to kill, Jake and Gerald took advantage of the time to get better acquainted, since they would be working closely together. To his relief, Jake found Gerald very pleasant company, always positive and optimistically forward-thinking albeit obviously a perfectionist so totally immersed in his work as to exclude life itself either by nature or because work was a form of escape for him from something he wasn't revealing. In trying to place his slightly different American accent, Jake learned that Gerald was Northeast establishment and indeed an Ivy League product—he'd gone to a prestigious prep school and then to Yale.

They did a bus tour of the city and for drinks and dinner settled for a steak house near the hotel on Moreno Street, where Jake said over coffee, "I can't get over how strange it always feels to be this far down in the southern hemisphere, like in Sydney or Brisbane, to say nothing of Tasmania."

"Oh? Strange how?"

"Disconnected. This big city of millions we're in now—it could be Rome or Paris, but most people back home can't remotely picture it. And this Catamarca where we change planes tomorrow. It's a sprawling city of two hundred thousand, I've read, and has to be filled with people like you and me—families, businesses, schools. It even has an important cathedral. Who the hell back home has ever even heard of it?"

"I agree. It just doesn't exist until you are actually here. I gather you've traveled a lot, Jake. How did you get into photography?"

"Backed into it. I was working as a camera operator for a New York television station owned by *The Daily News,* and late one night, between two shows, one of the news photogs came running into the studio wanting to know if anybody who could take pictures would fill the milkman stretch for him. His wife had just produced an heir or something like that. Well, there's no kinship between a TV camera, and the kind the news guys toted around back then when a guy virtually slept with a Speed Graflex. But I volunteered and found myself covering a nasty crime scene on Manhattan's Upper East Side in a squalid rundown tenement building with filth and rats everywhere and people shooting up and smoking crack on the stoop. A guy had murdered his wife, slashed her throat and then had hung himself in the bathroom. There was blood everywhere, and three terrified little kids were being taken care of by a woman cop. It was all death, but it was life, know what I mean? And I was so hooked. I never went back to television, and from then on it was anything that paid. How did you end up in management consultancy?"

Gerald grinned. "A little like you fell into photography. I was working for a small PR outfit that went broke and cut me adrift. But I was lucky; I got offered a management position with a run-down consultancy company I hadn't even applied to. I brought in a couple of blue-chip clients, and when I found myself running the joint, I bought it."

"That was it?"

"That was it. Gets me out and around a lot, and it has its perks. We're mostly tax-free in Geneva, and we can afford generous expense accounts. Are you married?"

"Divorced."

"Oh, sorry."

"Not a problem. It was friendly, believe it or not. How about you?"

"Very tied up, thank you."

"Do you live in Geneva?"

"No. Home is New York, and basically I'm there most of the time. Given modern communications, all I need in Geneva outside of winging over every month for a few days is a damn good office staff, and I have one."

"Does your wife work?"

"Never stops."

"What does she do?"

"Writes. Novels. Fiction."

"Hey, that's cool. Would I have read any of her stuff?"

"Probably not. Most of it is geared for women. She writes under her maiden name, Anders."

"Who?"

"Anders. Kelly Anders."

"Wait a minute, Gerald. Not *the* Kelly Anders."

"None other. I don't think there are two like Kelly." Gerald smiled broadly. "Anywhere."

"I guess not," Jake said. "I'm no great reader. My knowledge of writers usually has to do with the classics—people we had to read in college. Nowadays I'm too beat nights to read at all except crime fiction. But whenever I check the *Times* best-seller list to see what's new in that genre, your wife's name is always at the top of the better women's stuff."

"Yeah, she's been pretty successful."

"Where does she do her writing? I mean, does she have an office someplace, or does she work at home?"

"Mostly at home. She has a small cluttered-up room I'm forbidden to put a foot in even halfway. And then she totes around a laptop, and you can find her working almost any place. Like at dinner or when we're going someplace together and I'm driving. She never stops."

"I hope for bed, at least." Jake allowed himself a slightly insinuating smile.

"Oh, that, of course. Fortunately."

There was a sudden faint touch of resentment in Gerald's tone, and always sensitive to people's moods, Jake for the first time sensed a chink in Gerald's good-natured armor. He decided to change the subject and get out of Gerald's life, which he felt was really none of his business anyway. So he told a funny story about an elderly Vietnamese couple he'd met in Ho Chi Minh City when on a job for an American communications company. "They were running a secret business in pornographic literature," he said. "Their whole little house was filled with the dirtiest pictures imaginable. In their respectable old age, can you imagine?"

Turning in an hour later in his own room and after checking his cameras and equipment, Jake found himself wondering about Gerald, he and his famous wife. What with her writing and his endless backing and forthing trips to Switzerland and consulting trips far off like this one, what kind of a marriage? They clearly had little time together, only snatches of being a couple.

Thinking that, Jake began thinking about his own marriage. He hadn't told the truth when he'd said his breakup had been friendly. Janice had been viciously spiteful and unfair and had accused him of a thousand things that he'd never done but which she'd made up to influence a divorce judge and which he couldn't disprove. And all of that because he wasn't making enough money. He was a loser, she said. Trapped by his fear of the unknown into always taking the easier known route. And forever would be. Good photographers stayed in New York or London or Paris and did fashion shots or worked for PR outfits handling celebrities, like designers or film stars, and they cleaned up. In the end, no amount of money was good enough for her. She claimed he'd forced her to live in penury and wanted him stripped bare.

"She should have married someone like Alberto Castenelli," he thought. Screwed for money. Mostly, from what he'd seen around the world, the kind of women who flocked to a guy like the Italian—who, when you got right down to it, had nothing more to offer *than* money—were nothing more than whores. But that didn't bother a Castenelli, who probably was incapable of any sort of relationship deeper than a kids' plastic wading pool. A gorgeous young token wife whose job was to look beautiful and who only had to put out when he felt like it was good enough. In Geneva, when they'd met, the Italian's scorn for struggling miners whose lives were desperately hard, no matter in what country they worked, labeled him as lacking any real feeling.

Which is what, Jake thought, was so puzzling about the rather plain Jane the Italian had dragged along, because it was becoming clear from her expensive personal grooming and her designer suit and baggage that she wasn't just his secretary-cum-travel agent. She seemed well-educated, too. She spoke Italian like a native and some acceptable English. She'd spoken French to a French passenger on the plane. She was Lebanese or perhaps Egyptian in origin, Gerald said he'd heard, before becoming Italian. Gerald had also confided something he'd learned from a friend, who'd been at a urinal next to one Castenelli was using, that the Italian had never developed sexually. His penis was like a little child's.

Jake got out a map of Argentina and took it to bed along with his laptop. Christ, he thought, this Fiambala, when he'd finally found it and where the Argoronorte mine was located, is the back of fucking beyond. There didn't seem to be another town for a hundred miles, and a picture he pulled up on his laptop showed it lay on the edge of a rather foreboding desert and badlands, separated westward from the rising wall of the towering snow-capped Andes by tortured treeless foot hills, virtually mountains in themselves. Surrounding the town were occasional verdant clumps revealing lakes or hot springs. Well, if he could stay out of the Italian's hair, Gerald Evarts, for all his Ivy League-ness, was fair enough company. He'd found the Argies surprisingly European rather than Latin, and nothing lasted forever. Two or three weeks of photographing everything going, rats, cats, even the occasional vicuna or llama that strayed down from Bolivia or across the Andes from Chile, and he'd be back in civilization and then on to the next job. That could be Tibet, possibly. *Time* magazine wanted some special coverage of life in a monastery there.

"A damned nomadic monk," he thought. "That's me." With that he threw away the map, got out a beat-up notebook in which he kept a log of every job he did, and briefly scrawled in the events of the day.

FOUR

❧ ❦

*K*elly stared with something akin to anxious disbelief at the monitor of her laptop resting on the pull-out table in front of her and leaned back only long enough to have a sip of the icy margarita the air hostess in first class had lodged in the armrest's glass holder. Marcus, for Christ's sake, was starting to read like a nasty. How the hell had that happened? In the dialogue scene with Susanne, maybe? When Susanne got frosty because he had inadvertently become too involved for her liking in conversation with the real estate bitch? How far back was that, anyway?

She scrolled up until she found it in the previous chapter and read what she'd written. Oh, of course! Susanne's low-key attempt to extract Marcus before he gave away their negotiating hand had produced a far too irritable response, barely concealed by his forced smile. Completely un-Marcus and a threat to how she'd carefully fitted him into the plot. She must have then unconsciously carried it through. Scrolling back down, she found another place a few pages on and then yet another where Marcus was either unnecessarily angry or condescendingly sarcastic. Why on earth had she done that? It wasn't the way the book was planned. Marcus wasn't supposed to take on a life of his own. It had to be fixed, and she suddenly felt too tired to do so.

She closed the laptop and leaned back with the margarita, tilting the seat to suit and stretching out her feet and legs up onto the chair's padded extension. They were still three hours from London. How she dreaded it. Not London. She loved London. Comparing it to New York was like comparing an erudite college professor to an uneducated car salesman. She'd thought several times to move there and would if it weren't for Gerald. The doctors had said he couldn't survive a move. And book signings were always exhausting. They always found her with a kind of nervous stage fright before each one: the women— rarely men—who gushed unembarrassedly about your writing, the women who wanted to give you *ideas* for your next book or tell you about the book *they* were writing, and the women who shoved a book at you as though an order to sign it or else. It wasn't the same as the spontaneous little group she'd encountered coming away from her interview with David Hahn. Planned book signings were just that—planned and unnatural, with people lined up as though at a lunch counter or post office. Lined up and demanding, no matter how surface polite they were. "You're here to sign books, so sign this one, no argument, *God damn it,* and *now.*" It was the price you paid for being on top of the world.

She'd tried to get out of it, but Arson had insisted, although she had to wonder what writers did before book signings became not only the vogue but obligatory. Dickens didn't do book signing. Shakespeare didn't. But as Arson had said, "Your adoring public, Kelly, is capable of forgetting you in a matter of weeks. Book signing keeps a hard core of readers happy and gives you the endless publicity to rake in new readers. In whatever town you visit, regardless of size, there are reading groups and the ever-present specter of Oprah to be exploited. It pays the bills, my love. Pays the bills."

Why on earth had she ever agreed to that rot, any of it? She sensed there was some reason hiding way in the back of her mind somewhere that she didn't want to think about and that gave her a vague sense of guilt, which made her restlessly uncomfortable.

Worse than the book signing, worse by far—she felt unrepressed anger surge up in her—was what Arson, damn him, had sprung on her the moment they'd taken off when it was too late to balk at the whole trip, the meeting he'd slyly arranged with that damned woman, the famous British writer. What was her name? Oh, yes. Rachel Sommerset. McKain had given her a two-page "briefing summary" of the Nobel winner's life and work that included a picture—a gray-haired, scholarly austere woman, in her late sixties at least, her late-in-life clothes distressingly out of style. Her Nobel prize work, an over one-thousand-page masterpiece titled *The Spoils of War*, had been compared to Leo Tolstoy's great *War and Peace*, and Kelly was dead sure that she would be patronizing and condescending the way only the British could be.

The renowned British author had been born, raised, and educated in Wales; her father was a respected but impoverished don tutoring philosophy at one of England's smaller brick universities. She had won a scholarship at Cambridge, had worked a spell as an editor on *Future*, a left-wing weekly newspaper, and, when she'd inherited a small sum upon a great-aunt's death, had launched into independent writing—magazine articles and essays in effete journals, mostly—before writing her first three successful novels and then her masterpiece.

In a long life of writing, Sommerset had written but four novels read mostly by those deep into major literature with an emphasis on left-wing sociology or existentialist theories. She'd also published a number of politically slanted short stories that were considered highly important. She was a regular contributor to *The London Review of Books*, the British intellectual snob equivalent of its New York sister publication, which published only the most erudite among the erudite.

A fresh surge of resentment swept Kelly. Sommerset was clearly one of those who lived in some sort of rarified atmosphere of artistic snobbery, far removed from ordinary people. Her four novels in a lifetime that were so lauded by critics were nothing compared to her own record of fifteen, seven of them *New York Times* best-sellers, and some five short stories for the *New Yorker*. Maybe Arson had it all wrong. Maybe instead of *her* benefiting from a meeting with Sommerset, it would be the other way around, with Sommerset rewarded by seeming to have an association with her.

Her anger burning like gall, she pushed the button for the hostess, and when the hostess came, asked for another margarita.

—➤◄—

The young Eurasian serving her was surprised. Margaritas were not wine, they were strong stuff, and her passenger was drinking a lot. A part-time premed student, studying on her days off and even whenever she could during flights, she took more than a usual airline interest in the passengers in her care. She knew who Kelly was, had even read one of her books, which she had thought pointedly overly romantic and not to her own literary taste. But given Kelly Ander's best-selling fame, emphasized by Kelly's clothes and jewelry, her slightly imperious attitude toward all the air crew, and her traveling first class, she had to wonder why, in spite of it all, the woman basically looked unhappy. Even in her slightly false smile as she accepted the third margarita, there was no joy. She doesn't like her life, the young hostess thought. Worse, for some reason she doesn't really like herself. And wondered why she didn't.

—➤✦◄—

Arriving in London, Arson McKain put himself and Kelly up at the five-star Connaught, and the next day, still vaguely jet-lagged, Kelly was escorted to the London book signing by Arson and by Clarissa Chatterly of Crossroads' London office, the woman whom Arson had put in charge of Kelly's account. An all-business and surprisingly young redhead who, in stark contrast to her very academic and slightly out-of-date stiff British character, was wearing the latest in Paris fashion. She had laid on an almost impossibly rigorous schedule of book signing, beginning with a preliminary day in London itself, and Kelly found herself signing books first at Selfridges in the morning then at Harrods in the afternoon.

By evening she was dead on her feet and almost wishing she was back in New York, imprisoned with Gerald. After dinner with Clarissa and Arson at London's latest *in* place, where there was more chic and "the place-to-be-seen" than good food, she begged off any more book talk and retired to her hotel room, planning on a good night's sleep. Coming up were a last two days of freedom she'd insisted on. She would meet again with both publishers, put up with Chatterly's tourist guide chatter, and do some shopping—something wonderful for Estella and token presents, Fortnum and

Mason jams or chocolates, for the nurses. The following day and evening would be for work, and then she'd be off first for Edinburgh in Scotland. Coming back south, she'd sign books in the principal bookstores in Glasgow, Manchester, Birmingham, and Cardiff in Wales before finally returning to London to meet with Rachel Sommerset.

She had raided the minibar for a nightcap and barely removed her shoes when the phone rang. "Oh, damn it, Arson, enough is enough," she muttered when she went to answer.

But it wasn't Arson, it was the concierge. "Your concierge here, madam. There's a gentleman come in would like to see you if you haven't already retired. A Mr. Barlow."

The name first made no sense. Barlow? Who the hell was that? And then, when suddenly remembered, it hit Kelly like a hammer. In an instant nothing seemed real. "I … I'm sorry, who?"

"A Mr. Barlow, Madam. Would you like to speak to him?"

"Yes, yes, of course." Words that sputtered from her uncontrolled.

"One moment, please, Madam."

Distant telephone lobby sounds and then, "Kelly?" The voice from so long ago and yet strangely familiar.

"Jake? Oh, my God!"

"I'm in London and heard you were. Got time for a late drink?"

Hesitant but drawn as though by a magnet, "Yes.

Yes, of course I do. I 'll be right down."

"You'll find me in the bar."

Getting her shoes back on took what had to be a lifetime. She suddenly felt a weight on her chest that made it hard to breathe. She didn't bother to check her makeup. If she remembered Jake correctly, he wouldn't care how she looked. There was the carpeted hall outside her room when her legs felt like they were held back by rubber bands, there was the silent elevator, taking her down, but oh so slowly, slowly down and uncomfortable with two other stiffly silent people. And then the lobby and, her heart pounding and numb with a kind of almost frightened anticipation, she saw him, waiting by the door to the bar, his clothes looking no different than he had three years ago when he'd brought Gerald back from Argentina: the same worn cargo pants, the same faded denim shirt and worn corduroy jacket, the same uncut and undisciplined dark hair and two-day stubble.

She went to him and managed a welcoming smile and said, "Oh, my God, Jake. What a surprise!" She seized both his hands after a perfunctory kiss on his weathered cheek, and not knowing what to say, she said, "Where have you been? How on earth did you find me?"

"Kelly, gal. Finding you is a cinch. Just say 'Anders' and you're led right to her."

Still holding his hands, Kelly stepped back to look at him, at his chunky, rugged build. He had put on weight and was growing gray but, yes, he was the same

Jake who had got off the ambulance plane at Kennedy with Gerald. He had the same brutal jagged gash from his nose to his ear where a machete had caught him back in Argentina, a flaming red back then with twenty surgical clamps still in it. And his blinded left eye, lost to a rifle butt blow, an ugly gaping wound where the eye had been. Now both were pale scar tissue, the eye socket a mute, sunken place.

Jake laughed at an expression of concern she was unable to hide. "Doorman thought I was Dracula, almost didn't let me in."

"Never mind that. Where have you been? What have you been doing?"

Over drinks at a corner table in the now nearly empty bar, he filled her in: four months in the Congo for a drug company, six on a seagoing tug for Greenpeace, three months for CNN in Syria, two months doing portraits of executives at Volkswagen in Germany, a season at various Formula One races for a tire company, and the rest freelancing for various news agencies both in Europe and the USA.

"*Time* magazine did a feature page on your work based on what you did on race cars. They called it 'Racing the World.'"

"Did they? Too busy to find out. Guess I'm a hopeless rolling stone. So what about you? Best sellers one after the other, I hear. And Gerald?" He covered one of her hands with his and fixed her with a steady look. "I'm told he's still in a coma."

"Yes, I'm afraid so." It was a jolt when he suddenly

asked her—she'd become so immersed in his lifestyle—although she knew he would almost have had to.

"And what kind of hell is that? For you, I mean."

"The numb kind, Jake, and it's not really a coma, or not the usual kind, anyway. They're still getting un-coma-like brain responses. But otherwise he's like every part of him had had a stroke, though it's not that either. They really don't know what it is. They don't even know whether he hears or not. The brain neurologists. He doesn't seem to. He just lies there, motionless, staring. He's fed intravenously and is terribly thin."

"But you don't like to take the chance that he *can* hear and so you keep him. Just in case?"

"Something like that. Yes. We *were* married, after all."

"With all the pain that must still be there?"

"In a way." Kelly hesitated, then said, "Jake, what was she like? I mean *really*." She looked away, suddenly hating herself for asking. But then she said, "You're the only one I can ask who knows."

"Castenelli probably does."

"Castenelli? From the one letter I got from Gerald before it all happened, he probably never did. Apparently he had a problem."

"That department, true." Jake was thoughtful a moment, jiggling the ice in his drink. "Are you really sure you want to know, Kelly? I mean what she was like?"

"Yes."

"But why? It could only make the hurt worse, no?"

"No. Well, maybe. But at least she'd have an identity. Now she's like a shadow. Nobody or anyone or anything I can point to. No face, no voice. Just a meaningless name." She broke off in frustration. Then, "What *was* her name, anyway. I've forgotten it."

"Teresa."

"That's Catholic."

"I guess. Does that somehow make any difference?" When Kelly didn't answer, he said carefully, "Actually she was very ordinary."

A thought flared. Ordinary? Perhaps Gerald's infidelity would have been a little less unacceptable if she had been someone like herself. Someone who counted for something.

She heard Jake say, "And decent enough to feel terribly uncomfortable with Castenelli."

She said, "Well, if, as Gerald wrote me, Castenelli was impotent, why wouldn't she have been? Uncomfortable, I mean."

"I don't think it was the sex business. She might even have been grateful for the fact. That he couldn't, I mean. I had the impression she was with him only because she was desperate for a job. Any job. She had personal problems, apparently, a lot of debts."

"Millions of women have personal problems. And debts. They don't all whore themselves."

They were both silent a moment, interrupted by the bartender asking if they wanted a refresher. Jake ordered another round, and then Kelly said, "I don't think she sounds very nice at all. And being *ordinary* makes it harder than ever to understand. Gerald had better taste than ordinary, especially in women. He liked glamour in them—beauty and chic—just the way he liked the good life, expensive things and expensive surroundings. I gave him all of that with my success. And his, too, I guess, not to be grudging. I mean, we were fine."

"Were you? Sure?"

The way Jake said it, the challenge in his tone, caught Kelly unprepared. For a moment she could only stare. Then she said. "Jake, what are you trying to say?"

"I don't know, exactly, except I had the impression sometimes that he was rather lonely."

"Lonely? Gerald?"

"We had a talk once, my marriage, his. Mine was a bust. Maybe I had that impression because he said you worked so hard and he did, too, that you didn't have much time together."

Kelly laughed. "He said that? Shame on him, but it's probably true. However, that's life today, right? We're not in the nineteenth century any longer. Or the eighteenth. We're in the twenty-first and it's all high-tech and fast. You have to work like a hamster in its wheel just to stay in place. Of all people, you know that. So did Gerald. He worked overtime himself. Compulsively and from the day we met. I mean, I suppose that might have been a problem of sorts—like with millions others—but whenever we were together, it wasn't."

Jake made wet spiraling circles with his glass on the

tabletop. "I didn't mean no time together in the literal sense, Kelly."

"But what other sense?"

"I'm not sure. Maybe that somehow you were no longer in his life or he in yours."

Kelly stared at him. She sensed he was holding something back. She wasn't sure, but she began to feel a darkness creeping through her, a strange fear, as though opening a door to a forbidden room and terrified of what she might see.

"Jake ..." She heard her own voice as though from miles away and tried not to sound rudely shutting-out. "Let's change the subject, okay?"

He backed off awkwardly, slightly embarrassed. "Sure. Sorry if I've upset you. I'm no psychiatrist. I could be a hundred miles off base."

Kelly reached out and put her hand over his. "You haven't upset me, Jake. I— It's just that I've really tried to bury the past. Tell me what you did with Greenpeace."

He took the cue and told her about riding a fast-moving rubber boat after a Japanese whaling vessel, trying to get close enough for a shot of the crew on the ship's fantail and having a canon-fired harpoon lanced into them for their pains, sinking them into the icy water and being rescued just in time by their own mother ship. He laughed, remembering. "Cold? Oh, my God. They had me wrapped in a dozen blankets for days."

When it became very late, he wrote down how Kelly could get in touch with him if she ever wanted to. For both, it was oddly hard to part. Although not acquainted enough actually to call themselves friends, they had shared something that had created a bond between them that no amount of time or distance could erase. Back in her room after they'd said good-bye and she'd watched him cross the lobby and disappear into the dark maw of nighttime London, she felt a little badly at so clearly cutting him off. She tried not to think of the horror he must have suffered while held captive. Nor what Gerald must have suffered. She couldn't bring herself to think of the woman. Gerald's infidelity blotted out any thoughts about her and what she also must have been through.

She took a hot shower as though that would wash it all away, and then, after raiding the minibar again, she got into bed, trying to yield to merciful oblivion but lying awake a long time mulling over meeting Jake after so long a time and wondering if she'd been glad to see him or not. He'd brought back so many memories she'd thought she'd erased and now knew she never had. She wondered if she ever would.

FIVE

✦

Out in London's nighttime, Jake passed on going straight back to his own hotel. Walking restlessly, avoiding some still crowded streets, he found himself eventually seated on a bench in one of the many private gardens in London's West End that were surrounded by tall pale Georgian residences. A shadowed lawn with flower beds and shrubbery stretched out before him, silent now and perfuming the air with the smell of fresh cut grass. During the day, it would be filled with laughing children cautiously eyed by mothers and nannies chatting on benches and guarding infants in prams.

Remembering the stricken woman who had greeted him and Gerald at the airport on their return from Argentina, he had thought his meeting with Kelly would be only a pleasant and temporary courtesy call of sorts. Instead, it had left him strangely upset, forcing unwanted questions into his mind he couldn't easily shed—first about her and then, because of her, about himself.

He saw it unnaturally strange that she kept a barely alive Gerald, a virtual nonentity, in her New York apartment when he was quite certain from talks with Gerald, while held captive, that she had never loved Gerald, or perhaps so taken him for granted that she might as well have not. And that Gerald had felt this—that it was one reason why he so often strayed. Her continued pretense that she and Gerald "were fine together" had intensely irritated him—he'd hardly got that impression from Gerald—and made him somehow feel an involvement he couldn't shake off.

It was like her instant rejection of Teresa. A conventional response to be expected if she'd loved Gerald but false if she actually hadn't. He'd felt guilty for not rising more to Teresa's defense. He remembered how he had quickly come to see her not as Kelly did but as a woman who had somehow got on the wrong track in life, as so many so often did when uprooted for some reason from their origins, and was paying a bitter price for it. Whatever she had been before taking up with Castenelli and *why* she had taken up with the despicable Italian were obliterated by the person revealed when captive, a lost and lonely person of decency and warmth while fallen in grace from her religion but one with what was always important to him in other people—courage, or the lack of it. In her case there was enough courage, he had learned, for a dozen.

Thinking on his meeting with Kelly and her marriage, which had somehow got lost ever since Argentina in the glamour of her literary success, had forcibly and inevitably brought his thinking to himself in comparison. Didn't he also cover with a false aura of success what he more and more reluctantly recognized was the mess of his own life? He had touted up adventure—Greenpeace, Syria, all his travels and dangers—to Kelly, as he did to everyone. Wasn't he convincing himself that the role of the world-roving photojournalist was ideal when it wasn't? When it hardly was the glamorous life he was habitually painting it to be? It was a life of lonely isolation, one of meaningless defiance that must have started way back in rebellion against the appalling monotony and *correctness* of his father and mother's life—his father loyally sticking to the same spirit-numbing, petty, clerical job at the Ford factory in Detroit, year in, year out, to the point where he himself, watching it, had rebelled against anything even remotely similar that might have been even a happier and less constricted route to the inevitable restriction of the grave than the one he was on.

Jake could painfully remember the endless lecturing of his father not to yield to any romanticism of youth but to "hold fast to the plow," his favorite expression, and settle into a job after school that would spell security for his lifetime. With that surged the memory of the day in college when, inspired by what had seemed to him the gloriously liberal and rebellious thought of a professor in a humanities course, he had made up his mind that he'd be damned in hell before he followed in his father's footsteps.

Now, sitting on the bench in the near dark, the only light coming from within the graceful Georgian buildings surrounding the garden, he thought of the people in some who lived family lives of interest and security. He'd somehow missed the boat, he knew, and he felt suddenly overcome with loneliness. The road ahead no longer looked welcoming. It looked bleak and alien. Roving the world, feeling independent and beholden to no one but himself had worn itself out. The thought of his being once again off on his own, to some unknown and utterly unfamiliar place, appalled. The endless traveling, the forever sordid second-class hotel rooms, struggling always with languages that were not his own, his meeting and working with strange people, his forming fleeting friendships that would disappear like the mist the moment the job was finished, his forever returning not to a home and the familiar, but to yet another unknown place and unknown people— all that, which was his life, had become impossible. And yet the thought of change seemed too daunting to contemplate. He felt he no longer had the strength or the will. He had waited too long. Janice had urged him to open his own photography studio someplace— Geneva, or Rome, or Paris, or even New York. He'd balked. Why? Because it was Janice who'd suggested it? Perhaps, but it was too late now.

He thought again of Teresa. Her life had been something like that. No anchor anywhere, apparently.

He'd been mildly envious of Gerald, he remembered, when she had seemed to think Gerald a haven of some sort from Castenelli. Jealous, actually, but why? Not because Gerald was in for a romp in bed, he realized, but because Gerald, while surely unknowing, because sex was all that was on Gerald's mind, was taking over a woman who had so far missed out on everything that, sitting there in the near darkness, he himself had now begun to see desirable. The memory of Gerald's impersonal use of Teresa way back then in Argentina made him now regret even more his own years of casual one-night pickups in bars, his loveless agreements with those he met at work or at cocktail parties. Argentina had made him more than ever aware of his own lost innocence.

He wondered what had happened to Teresa. It had been bitter to abandon her, but he'd had no choice. He'd heard she had finally been rescued by the soldiers and hoped she'd recovered from her terrible injuries. Had she been insured in any way? He doubted Castenelli had had the common decency to include her in his own insurance nor, certainly, that she'd had enough money herself to insure against such an awful happening. For if indeed she could have afforded insurance, he was quite certain she would not have been so desperate as to work for Castenelli, which had to have been for her the ultimate in degradation.

He thought of Kelly again. Rich and successful and living with a near corpse. Did her life make any sense either? Try as he could, it was hard not to picture it.

After a while and as lights in some of the surrounding Georgian buildings began to wink out, Jake rose and headed for his own hotel, one that was a far cry from Kelly's Connaught. He'd perhaps try some day to locate Teresa. She had to be someplace, and he owed her at least the brief visit he had given Kelly.

It had been a trying evening. With his footsteps sounding on the silent pavement of the empty street beyond the square, he began to think of his next assignment.

SIX

She signed books in her overcoat in the cold chill of Scottish Edinburgh when the heat in the garishly lit bookstore failed and while feeling oppressed the whole time by the contrasting gauntness of the centuries-old gray-stone Gothic buildings of the great university that towered over the city.

In Glasgow, she signed books when there was such a fog that it had even penetrated the bookshop itself with its awful chill, making her hand stiff with cold and it miserable to write her name even in a hasty scrawl.

In Manchester, she signed scores more to the blare of a background television that made it hard to hear the demands of those requesting a signature and where the constant interruptions of a football riot spilling from the stadium into the streets seemed to consume the bookstore employees as well as most of the city.

She signed books in Birmingham while Clarissa

Chatterly hovered about as usual like a dithering schoolmistress and trapped her into addressing a large women's reading group assembled in some important person's private residence that resembled more a funeral parlor in its decor than a home. She'd been kept there forever with one persistent woman aggressively demanding to know what she was *saying* in all her books as though every page had some hidden meaning. And afterward she'd had to pretend pleasure when served a tepid tasteless tea when she'd reached a point where she'd thought she'd die if she didn't have a margarita.

Finally, and with a perpetually frozen smile, she'd dutifully signed books in Cardiff after a miserable and chilly night in an unnecessarily shabby and icy hotel room where she'd not slept a wink and even after there'd been an ugly incident. A gaunt, gray-faced woman who hid her hair beneath a wide straw hat garnished with faded artificial flowers had shouted at her in a high, screaming, nearly unintelligible voice, denouncing her for blasphemy and for writing pornography, and then had set fire to the stack of books waiting to be signed. The fire put out, the woman led away, the remaining fog of smoke had forced her to sign books out on the pavement of a dismally unattractive street where there was soon such humid dampness as to make her feel soaked to the skin.

Throughout all of it, Kelly found herself haunted day and night—night was the worst—by Jake Barlow and what had happened in Argentina. She'd told Jake he hadn't upset her when the truth was that his unexpected appearance after three years had brought back what she'd nearly been successful in burying, the whole nightmare of Gerald's arrival: the airport, the chartered ambulance plane landing, Gerald coming off it on a gurney to the ambulance that would rush him with a police escort to the New York hospital, the crushing media, TV cameras pushing and shoving to get better and closer shots of the blanket-swathed man. And all the time herself torn between the stomach-wrenching shock of seeing his still unconscious form made worse and more real by Jake's brutal injuries while there'd been all the pain of Gerald's suddenly being the enemy and no longer Gerald, her husband, the guy she'd lived with and slept with for ten years but now a stranger who'd publicly shattered her self-esteem.

For weeks she hadn't been able to look at television. Every channel reveled in every aspect of what had happened. Nor could she pick up a newspaper. The ever relentless tabloids, relishing more in her husband's infidelity than his captivity by the dissident miners' group with all their mindless brutality, seemed unable to desist from endlessly rolling in every sordid aspect of the story.

And then, all the nightmare of having to bring him home from the hospital: the arrangements for nurses, the move to a new apartment from where she had felt comfortable and safe and the special room for Gerald, a special bed, the doctors, doctors, doctors, the wrangles with lawyers and insurance people, the coping with his distraught parents who somehow managed to insinu-ate it was all her fault. It had gone on and on and on. How could anyone write and live through all that? But she had. Writing became an escape.

Jake had done her no favor with his unexpected appearance. The months of numbness she'd carefully pushed away now all came back on her in a flood, a jumble of wounding, painful, and incoherent memo-ries and feelings: Gerald unfaithful, the moment he was away from her, rutting like an animal with some strange Italian woman. Why, why? My God, had he been doing the same before Argentina, stealing off secretly while she was at work to shack up in a hotel room someplace, or in some other woman's home—to be in some other woman's body and then coming back into their bed together to be in hers? With her trusting and oblivious? She couldn't stand it. It wasn't fair for that to be her lot. It wasn't. How could he have done that to her? But he had.

Thinking to dismiss thinking any more of Gerald, she tried to stop thinking of Jake, too, and all the mem-ories he'd brought back that she'd tried hard to forget. It wasn't easy, and dismally she realized that they would stay with her perhaps forever.

➤◄

Book signing finally over and on the way back from Cardiff by train with the ever-present Clarissa Chatterly ensconced reading one of her books on the seat opposite her in the first-class compartment, Kelly's thoughts were still on Jake and his sudden appearance. She couldn't undo having seen him again. What on earth had he meant when he said Gerald struck him as being *lonely*? Gerald had never seemed lonely. And he'd never *said* he was. How could he have been when he was almost never alone? When not working they were together almost all the time. He shared a bed with her, he had breakfast with her nearly every day, they dined together at night, shared bathroom and showers, vacationed together, went to parties and the theatre and movies and concerts together, enjoyed mutual friends, the sport club with herself on a treadmill, Gerald on an ellipse.

And all that almost from the day they met. How could he possibly have been lonely?

No. Jake had to be wrong. But why, then, had he said it? She tried to think. Okay, so suppose, just suppose, Jake was right but lonely somehow because of her, or had he always been lonely? Some people were, but that didn't seem possible with Gerald. He'd had a happy, trouble-free, spoiled childhood and school years before and during prep school and then Yale and scores of friends not just by his account but by his parents, who clearly doted on their son.

Before Argentina there had been numerous framed pictures of their happiness in their early years together, shots of them on beaches and at ski resorts, their wedding and themselves, the bridesmaids and maid of honor, and his best man along with pictures of his parents. She'd thrown them all out, but she couldn't get rid of memories as easily. Their meeting at a cocktail party from which he'd pulled her away early to dine at a neat Greenwich village bistro he loved and her first impression of someone far more handsome and intelligent than any she'd ever encountered before. Top drawer socially and seductive besides. He'd loaded her with champagne, and she hadn't been able to resist bed on their first date, nor for a long time after. They'd made love the night before he'd departed for Geneva to link up with Castenelli and go to Argentina.

She thought of his parents. She didn't like them. Their hostility barely masked, they'd never accepted her except superficially for appearances' sake. Now they'd decided she'd failed their son. Gerald never would have been unfaithful, she'd had to have pushed him to it. His father graying and self-important with all his success as an orthopedic surgeon and pride as a Yale alumnus where Gerald had succeeded him, Gerald's mother, middle-aged, always perfectly groomed and forever enjoying the self-inflicted martyrdom of all her do-good social activities. When she'd first met them and because of her own standing as a best-selling author, they hadn't dared express their disappointment on seeing Gerald was serious about her. Within minutes, they had decided he'd not made the "right" social choice they had expected of him, that he'd not picked someone of their own social class.

Their constrained questions about her own family, of whom they clearly suspected the worst, had amused her. Gerald had told them what she'd told him, that her fictitious parents had been killed in a car crash, but that didn't help their curiosity about her pre-author years, of her being raised by an aunt about whom they could find nothing (because no such aunt had ever existed) or the fact that she'd only done community college. Outwardly, she'd played the gracious act of the successful woman in the world of literature and publishing. Inwardly she'd laughed.

Gerald had, too. He was a free spirit, and he had no illusions about his parents' social snobbery. The fact that he didn't somehow made it seem even more impossible for him to be lonely. Every day for Gerald was a wide-open day to be enthusiastically challenged, to make plans and, as he often said, "to get the world by the tail." She'd often wondered, did he ever think of himself?

It seemed so odd that Jake had a whole different take on him. Had Gerald confided a side of himself to Jake he'd never revealed to her? Some complaint about her or some long hidden resentment at her success, perhaps? It was hard to think so. He'd always been totally supportive and enthusiastic about each new book, her endless time-consuming efforts. She tried to think of something she might have said and done that he had secretly resented and made him feel alienated and had kept to himself. She could think of nothing.

When's she'd signed a book and had handed it back, she always found herself wondering what secrets lay behind the reader's smile of grateful pleasure—or, as in

Cardiff, a snarl of rage and arson. You couldn't really know what someone else was actually thinking, not even a husband or a lover. You couldn't fathom a human mind if it didn't want to be fathomed. And even then, if seemingly revealed, you couldn't know what secrets were still carefully held back, locked away, never to be unlocked. What had Gerald held back where she was concerned that had burst out in Argentina?

❧❦

Thinking this way and when still an hour out of London, her thoughts were interrupted by the claxon sound of her cell phone demanding her attention. She scrambled it out of the mess in her shoulder bag. "Hello?"

It was Arson McKain, and he called to tell her that her meeting in London was off. Some friend of Rachel Sommerset had some sort of domestic problem, a sick dog or cat or something—he hadn't got it quite straight—that she had to tend to, apparently, and she couldn't manage the trip up from her country home near Chichester in the South Downs, so they had rearranged the meeting to be down there.

"Oh, for Christ's sake, Arson. I've had enough bloody travel."

"Sorry, love. Bear with it. You've been doing such great work so far. It's really paying off. I've laid on a limo and it's only an hour and a half drive. She said she'll take you to lunch at her local. A bit of old England, right? I'm sure you'll enjoy it."

"But Arson …"

"See you at the hotel tonight, Kelly. Bye." And he was gone.

"Shit!" Kelly said. Ignoring the questioning look of Clarissa Chatterly, she slung the cell back into her bag. *Local* meant a pub and she was in no mood for a pub's beery smell. It made meeting the English writer less formal and too social for her liking. On the damned woman's home turf, she'd be somewhat at a disadvantage since being a guest by nature always put one slightly on the defensive, a position she found intolerable. But promotion was promotion, and the money from it was money, a fact of life. She was stuck with it.

She was still having angry troubling thoughts when only a few minutes from London. She managed to push them back. Her hated book signing tour was over. What the Rachel Sommerset woman would be like and how she could avoid being in any way dominated by her didn't really matter. She'd be home before the week was up, the ordeal over and the whole book tour, the English novelist included, mercifully forgotten.

She turned to look out the window at the passing countryside.

➤◄

On the seat opposite, Clarissa Chatterly raised her eyes a moment from the book she was reading to glance across at her. From the moment she had met Kelly she had been distressed by a sense of inequality. The

American whom she escorted came from no place. She'd never had any education other than two years in a community college of dubious standing. There was even lesser value in her years in some working-class Chicago high school in spite of which she seemed to have performed some sort of miracle in getting herself started on a stellar writing career. She herself, in bitter comparison, Clarissa thought, while coming from a cultured upper-class background and a first-honors in reading English literature at one of the better brick universities, had got no place further than being a sort of superior gofer for the British branch of Crossroads Publishing. With no name and no publication record, her own first, secretively written novel about a fated love affair, which some friends thought quiet decent, had been returned by several agents she'd tried and gone nowhere.

Most infuriating was that behind the expensive clothes, the immaculate hair styling and makeup, the American seemed to have little interest in what she wrote and turned out her books almost mechanically in a clear formula that she stuck to. It made one wonder why she kept doing so. Envy of Kelly, in spite of herself, had risen so hard within Clarissa during the tour that at times she'd thought she wouldn't be able to continue.

She dreaded the meeting arranged with Rachel Sommerset. Jealousy of the Nobel winner even greater than what she felt about Kelly gnawed in her also. It was hard to be a nobody among the elite, to have to bow and scrape in order to keep body and soul together.

Life wasn't fair. She wanted to cry but knew that wouldn't do, not in any way. Misery was something you kept to yourself and hid with a cheery voice and a smile. You might hate your so-called betters but you didn't ever let them know it.

SEVEN

In Argentina, Jake felt comfortable that he was getting the shots of those around the dining table he'd been hired to do. The best shots were when people were unaware of being photographed and so far nobody had seemed to notice him except for Gerald, who caught his eye once and winked. It was their first night at the Argoronorte mine. The dining room was in the surprisingly modern two-story glass-and-brick administration building, the office domain of its engineers and geologists whose living quarters were in small neat rows of nearby Quonset huts, each with its tubs of flowers or shrubs by the door to help soften the harshly barren and arid surroundings of the mountainous Andean foothills and complete the overall tidy residential picture.

Juan Pablo Santiago, the mine's silver-haired and sun-bronzed general manager, had somehow managed to make the whitewashed breeze-block room in which they dined presentable for his distinguished overlord. The Italian, on his part, seemed barely able to hide his general discomfort at where he was and the need to rub elbows with underlings who, except for business requirements, he would hardly have deigned to notice. The other diners, Ian Carter-Wright, the surprisingly young engineer in charge of ore extraction, his British north-country origins written all over him as well as in his speech, and Carlos Olivares, a portly and older Argentinian engineer in charge of actually mining the ore containing gold, were clearly making an effort not to feel equal discomfort although at the same time enjoying the rarity of the luxurious food Castenelli had ordered trucked in from Catamarca for his stay.

The only person who seemed suitably relaxed was Gerald. He was seated next to Teresa, and the Italian's consort was having difficulty, Jake noticed, in not paying too much attention to him, which was, he suspected, the reason for Gerald's good humor. It made him suddenly wonder if Gerald was the type who, when away from home, could be a pushover for someone not his wife, even a plain Jane like Teresa. On the flight up from Buenos Aires—called the *capitale federale* by the Argentines—to Catamarca, where they had spent the night in a *parador,* an efficient government-sponsored hotel, she had begun to appear to Jake a little less ordinary. Beneath a quietly guarded exterior that he decided was mostly laid on for Castenelli, or perhaps *because* of the Italian, Jake sensed a certain well-sequestered sexuality that could, if unlocked, prove appealing. When Castenelli had retired early she had seemed quite a different person.

Early in the morning they'd then flown on a chartered helicopter from Catamarca to Fiambala, avoiding a tortured two hundred miles of narrow and empty tarmac road across expansively flat desert and badlands that were devoid of any sign of life save for one town that, surrounded by a bit of rare green, had suddenly appeared far beneath them as though simply dropped there in its alien entirety by mistake.

Jake had been excluded from the dinner. With some embarrassment Gerald had informed him that he wasn't to dine with management. The Italian saw a photographer, Gerald said, as being there only to take pictures. Jake, amused at the social snobbery rather than angry, had eaten earlier on a food-stained trestle table in a storeroom just off the kitchen along with the obsequious and forever nervous little valet, Gino, and some of the lesser Argoronorte employees. They were a mixed group, geologists and engineers who were Argies or Brits along with several he suspected of being Kosovars, a Balkan group who seemed, like the Scots once had, to be suddenly all over the world. One of the company, an Argentinian named Pepe de Pulmumarca, was there representing the miners. Rarely speaking and obviously feeling out of place in a stiff suit with shirt and tie which clearly he had rarely if ever worn, his hair cut high above his ears and the back of his neck for the occasion, he'd been invited from the miners' tin-roofed shantytown half a mile up the valley to meet and dine with Castenelli. The Italian, true to his nature, had canceled the invitation when told of it. Pulmumarca was to eat with the servants.

All during the course of the lesser-executive meal—soup, some over-boiled vegetables, some greasy, nearly raw, and unidentifiable meat—Jake reflected on the day from the moment the little town of Fiambala had suddenly appeared beneath them, a tiny oasis pushed up against the jagged and darkly menacing barren foothills of the giant Andes. Waiting for the transport that would take them to the mine, he and Gerald had explored the area and surrendered for an hour to the luxury of one of the many hot springs in and around the town that was bustling with tourists and cyclists. While they did, an irate Castenelli had tried to get the helicopter pilot to fly him to the mine immediately—a vain request. Mountain storms and violent air currents in the area that day made flying there excessively dangerous.

The trip was made instead in the two company SUVs and was slow torture. The narrow and rutted dirt road was steep, crowded in on by walls of the towering treeless foothills and sometimes edging along precipitous drops of a hundred feet or more while strewn with fallen rock that in frequent stops had to be removed before they could proceed. At other times, the squeeze past Argoronorte trucks coming their way was heart-stopping. The forty-odd miles took three hours, and Jake's only solace was that Castenelli, whom he had begun to thoroughly dislike, was suffering equally.

Although used to rough travel, he was beginning to be completely fed up himself when the narrow pass suddenly opened surprisingly onto a deep valley that seemed mostly filled with a large conglomerate of sprawling factory buildings, some with windows and some the open sides of which exposed heavy machinery. The SUVs headed for the modern administration building but not before Jake had seen the large, yawning hole, halfway up a precipitous slope, that was the entrance to the tunnel mine itself and where, on a wide shelf, a backhoe was lifting rock from rail cars just exited the mine and dumping the contents onto a chute to roar and rattle down to a huge rock crusher below. Farther up the valley where it was sunless and narrowed back into a dark canyon, he also saw the clusters of miserable tin-roofed shacks that were the homes of the actual miners.

Castenelli, still sheet white from fear and with a handkerchief to his face against a pervasive stench of chemicals that filled the valley, was immediately greeted and ushered into one of the larger Quonsets by Juan-Pablo Santiago, the general manager. He was followed with obvious reluctance and a backward glance toward Gerald and himself by Teresa, who left Gino to struggle with Castenelli's extensive baggage. Jake and Gerald were whisked by a cheerful north-country Ian Carter-Wright onto a terrace outside the administration building for a beer and sandwich lunch and then taken on a tour of the sprawling gold extracting facilities.

Jake had never had much interest in any sort of manufacturing, let alone extracting gold from endless chunks of rock ferreted from someplace far underground, in the case of the Argoronorte mine, rather than from some vast open pit. He found big industrial machinery a ready subject, however. Photography of it could impart artistry besides a sense of imposing, even awesome strength. It could give an individual monster mass of steel and iron a personality. While Ian Carter-Wright explained an intricate process to an enthralled Gerald, he caught only enough words to digest a simplistic version of the whole gold extraction process, which he was to write in his notebook that night. The mined rock was crushed into a fine powder, and turned into a virtual soup with a mixture of water and cyanide, which separated the gold-bearing liquid from the rest of the soupy mix. That liquid was then infused with carbon particles which further isolated the gold itself. The gold was then removed in turn from the carbon by thousands of degrees of furnace heat and, as ninety-percent-pure ingots, was shipped away someplace to be made nearly a hundred percent pure by a complex electric process.

Castenelli retired almost immediately after dinner that night, followed by an again reluctant Teresa. Jake and Gerald, before going to their own assigned Quonset hut, went with Ian Carter-Wright and some geologist and engineers to a sort of common room whose cement block walls were starkly bare save for a bulletin board and some pinup-girl posters and where there were two sagging couches, shabby stuffed chairs, and a TV monitor atop a stunted cold drinks refrigerator.

➤◄

In the living room of his VIP Quonset hut, carefully prepared for his visit with a decor to match a five-star hotel, and while Teresa waited in silence for whatever his wish, and Gino, in one of the two adjoining bedroom suites, laid out pajamas on the king-size bed, Castenelli poured himself a scotch and soda at a well-stocked drinks table. Finally breaking an almost ominous silence, he said to Teresa, "Between the drive to get here and having to suffer dinner with the employees, I won't need your services tonight." And, without even looking at her, he went into the bedroom, taking his drink with him and closing the door firmly behind him.

Doing so, he missed the look of amused contempt that followed him. Making sure he wasn't coming back, Teresa went to her own smaller bedroom and in the bathroom washed her hands and then almost compulsively washed them a second time. Ever since she'd become a sex therapist, washing hands had become an endless ritual. She washed them before she met with a client and afterward even if she never touched them but especially on the rare occasion when she'd had to.

Like Castenelli, she was beginning to find this trip far into northern Argentina exhausting. But not for the same reasons. It was Castenelli himself who was wearing her out. She was beginning to so thoroughly dislike him that any personal contact with him was abhorrent even when there was no talk of sex with erotic pictures to be pored over, or no hard-core porn to be watched together on her iPad.

How had she ever got into this profession, she wondered? If you could call it a profession. It was worse than before she'd wangled an Italian passport and got herself out of Lebanon, where life had been a blur of unwanted men and lousy jobs to keep herself alive. In the melting pot of Beirut, where there was every nationality and every sort of human, a very old man said he had known her father and that her parents had been Kurdish refugees from Turkish oppression. But she couldn't remember her parents and would never know if that was true or not.

And then the promised land of Italy had been a bust, too—bad jobs, bad men, Italian prejudice against immigrants. A friend had persuaded her sex therapy was good money, and she'd borrowed enough to buy a phony degree that said she was a psychologist and which gave her hope of finally earning a decent living.

"It will get you twice what you can make with normal patients and half the work, Teresa. It's not like prostitution. You're not selling yourself. You're selling knowledge, you're a psychologist sorting out some stupid guy's sexual hang-ups. And you don't ever have to put out unless in some rare case you might find you wanted to."

Since she'd started, she'd run through a dozen clients, wondering more and more with each one what it was that had caused it to all go so wrong with so many of the male sex. Then someone had recommended her to Castenelli. He was only the second she'd ever actually had to touch, and it had utterly repulsed her. It wasn't because he had never developed. She could somehow bear that by forcing herself to think professionally. It was the nonsexual Castenelli that colored everything physical, his heartless arrogance that she hated. In Catamarca, she'd decided the Italian would be her last ever client. She hadn't opted out back there because he was paying her enough money to never have to do sexual therapy again. What the hell, Teresa, she'd thought. It's only a couple more weeks and you're through with all of it forever.

She dried her hands and left the bathroom, got out a nightie from her suitcase and then suddenly wondered why she was going to bed; she wasn't all that tired and didn't have to. The guys, Gerald and the photographer and some of the engineers and geologists, were all having a drink in what was laughingly called their lounge and talking and having fun. She said to herself, "Well, why not? He's out for the count." Impulsively, she unpacked a new basic-black linen dress, held it up, and decided it was okay for the wilderness, even if a little low-cut, and maybe that was a good idea because she'd seen Gerald had an eye on her and, married or no, he was a hundred percent cute, and she felt starved for romance. She put it on, liked the mildly sexy way it looked, and then added evening makeup and quietly left the hut.

❧

They had only finished first beers, and Ian Carter-Wright was opening up a new twelve pack when Teresa suddenly reappeared, causing a minor sensation. Plain Jane had metamorphosed into a rather pretty woman, the designer suit replaced by a low-cut sleeveless dress over which she'd casually tossed a cardigan that failed to hide an appealing bosom, and she had applied makeup and perfume. Deprived for long periods of female company, Carter-Wright and friends were goggle-eyed, and although she gave a semblance of flirtatiousness with all of them, it was clear to Jake that she actually had eyes only for Gerald.

"It's definitely on," he thought when, slightly disenchanted, he saw Gerald responding. It made him wonder how they planned to hide an affair, if it came to that. Castenelli, although an asshole *aristo*, was not stupid and would be bound to notice. That led to a flood of questions and speculation. What was the woman's relationship with the Italian? Given his reported sexual condition, was she indeed his mistress as everyone seemed to take for granted she was? Or wasn't she, and just a convenient secretary to be bullied about the same way he bullied his poor valet? If she wasn't his mistress, would the Italian care that she was having an affair with someone he felt beneath him and feel perhaps personally tainted by it? Or if she actually *was* his mistress, and they were somehow able to have sex, did they have some sort of kinky arrangement in which he vicariously enjoyed her sex with others, or worse, even encouraged it? Jake had run into a few like that over the years.

"Well," he thought, "time will tell." And what about Gerald's writer wife? Was their perfect marriage actually on thin ice? Or was this simply the case of a husband taking liberties when away from home that were basically not meaningful and typical of a marriage so superficial and shallow in meaning that infidelity to one or both was nothing that engendered any deep pain or guilt. Having never met Kelly Anders, there was really no way of knowing. Her celebrity status would certainly hide what her relationship with Gerald really was. But actuality would surface sooner or later, he thought. It always did.

EIGHT

❖

*J*ake had always been bad at confined spaces. The moment he was shut in a small room, either by accident or on purpose, he would immediately feel claustrophobic. Mines were the one danger in all his years of world roaming that he had always managed to avoid. Now, stuck with going into one, he could only thank the heavens that the Argoronorte mine was straight into the mountain, nearly a mile of horizontal tunnel that branched off twice into two long, secondary tunnels, equally horizontal, and that it was not one of those South African ones that took you straight down five thousand feet in an elevator. That sort of visit would have done him in completely.

Young Carter-Wright had announced to him and Gerald at breakfast that Carlos Olivares, the pleasantly smiling and portly mining chief, would take them, along with himself, into the mine as soon as they finished their coffee. And so before he could gird on his mental armor, Jake, cameras slung about his shoulders, found himself following the three men up a steep ladderlike stair to the wide rock shelf at the yawning void of the mine's entrance. There the huge, precariously perched backhoe was lifting rock from one of several rail cars, pushed from the mine on a narrow rail track by a small electric engine, and dumping the rock onto the wide conveyor chute he'd seen on arriving to be carried down to the giant rock crusher far below, the thunderous grinding noise of which filled the valley. One of the rail cars, a flat bed, had four benches bolted onto it. Seated, Jake found himself pulled into the humid darkness of the dreaded tunnel, the daylight that flooded its yawning entrance fast diminishing into a mere prick of distant light before there was oppressive darkness relieved only by the occasional flat glow of widely spaced wall lights and by the flaring headlight on his hard hat and those of the others.

Castenelli had deferred a visit and would depend for any knowledge of the actual mining operation on Gerald's report and the photos Jake took. So Jake almost at once somehow managed to hold down his claustrophobia. As the little engine dragged them farther and farther into the mountain, he started firing off shots of everything from shadowy groups of miners they passed in places where the tunnel widened, to the complex, heavy timbering that prevented a cave-in and the long ventilating pipes attached to the tunnel walls.

He had exhausted subject matter when, after enduring for half a mile the deafening high-pitched whine from the rail engine and the jarring rattle of the cars' wheels on the rail tracks, they finally arrived at the end of the tunnel. There, in a suddenly opened space, he was assailed by a new cacophony of sound as helmeted sweating miners, stripped to the waist and with most wearing protective eye shields, attacked the tunnel walls with compressed-air jackhammers as well as with picks and mining bars.

The moment the train stopped, a small backhoe immediately began loading the piles of rock loosened by the miners onto the cars, and Jake with the three others got down off their benches. They had hardly done so when one of the miners, body hair matted with rock powder and sweat, broke loose from a group of others and approached them. He was a stocky powerful man with a rocking gait from a once leg injury, and because of his hard hat, his lack of an ill-fitting rarely worn suit and fresh workman's haircut, Jake didn't immediately recognized him as Pepe de Pulmumarca, the head miner and their representative.

His small hooded eyes, burning with anger, swung over the group of visitors, taking them in, and without waiting for any sort of introduction he assailed Olivares and Carter-Wright in coarse Spanish.

"Where's that son-of-a-bitch Castenelli?" And without waiting for an answer, "Slopping up wine at breakfast on a white table cloth, probably. Too damn dangerous and dirty in here for the likes of him. Didn't take but one look to get his shit-face Italian measure last night. Miners making his money for him are too far beneath him to share a meal." Pepe Pulmumarca had hardly forgotten Castenelli's dinnertime snub.

Olivares was quietly firm. "Calm down, Pepe. You're talking about the boss and your meal ticket. He's on a call with board members discussing things that can only be to your benefit."

Which Jake knew was not true. More likely Castenelli was indeed taking his leisure, although more likely in bed with coffee than at breakfast drinking wine. As Olivares continued to placate the irate head miner and then explain to Gerald and Carter by showing with rock samples how the geologists knew they were in on a vein of gold, he found his mind wandering. Last night had ended after an hour of laughter and beer exactly as he'd thought it would, with Gerald in bed with Teresa. He had heard them sneak quietly into the Quonset he shared with Gerald sometime after he was comfortably half asleep. He'd heard their muted voices, the hint of laughter, and then after a few minutes the faint but unmistakable sounds of sex, a man's increasing exertion and a woman's muffled ecstasy. Later he heard her slip quietly away.

It made him uncomfortable. Not so much for Gerald personally, although he thought it pretty risky and a behavior that somehow diminished Gerald, stripping him of respect and authority. But for Jake, there was more than that. Marital infidelity had always disturbed him. He'd suffered enough, Lord only knew, from the often blatant affairs that Janice had indulged in and then had defiantly accused him of to help her gain more money in their divorce. He had learned the hard way that once the bond of trust is broken, whether by man or woman, and even if fences are mended, something goes out forever of what held them together. The breech leaves the injured party with an insecurity, a sense of vulnerability and exposure to all life's other dangers that was far greater than any amount of indignation or anger could heal.

The rapidity with which Gerald had seduced or been seduced by Teresa left Jake again wondering about the state of Gerald's marriage. Did he love his wife at all? Did his high-powered author love him? What kept them together? Convention? Habit? The often economic disaster of divorce held at bay by pretense? Gerald's enjoying Teresa most certainly could not have been his first infidelity. Jake suspected that other women with Gerald was chronic, and he also suspected that no matter how good the sex was or wasn't that Gerald had little feeling about the woman he shared it with, whomever she might be.

Coming back from inspecting the mine shaft, he thought it all a shame. Teresa actually seemed more and more a very nice person. He saw her as one of those who'd somehow missed the boat, had got left behind in life and was hard put to keep her head above water. But there was a natural warmth in her, and he suspected she had gone to bed with Gerald with less selfishness than he with her. Regardless of his morals,

Gerald Evarts was a very attractive guy with a lot going for him, and he'd come on to her pretty strong. And what about Castenelli? Did he know, or suspect? If he and Teresa shared a bed and if he hadn't wondered at her going out after they had retired, then he had to have wondered even more why she was so late in coming back. Unless, of course, they had some sort of an arrangement which, he thought, given Castenelli's apparent genital infantilism, could be quite possible.

He was snapped out of further speculation by finding himself covering a conference between Gerald, Olivares, Carter-Wright, the general manager Pablo Santiago, and Castenelli himself. The Italian was clearly but recently up and dressed, as evidenced by his still damp hair and the odor of shaving lotion and men's perfume. Jake found it hard not to draw comparison between the chairman and his world of wealth and power and the miners he'd seen sweating in the cramped area at the end of the mine shaft. One was so hopelessly distant from the other.

Castenelli was saying, "Get rid of him. He's out of line. This thug of yours … what's his name?"

"Pulmumarca. Pepe Pulmumarca."

"Whatever." Castenelli waved a dismissive hand. "We're not dealing with him. He wants more pay, he can speak through his union down in Buenos Aires."

Olivares said, "I'm afraid it's not that easy, sir. That could take forever. Meanwhile, the miners' living here is substandard and hard on them. Many are far from their families, and we could find ourselves in a precarious situation if Pepe got it in his head to pull them all off the job."

"I'm not interested in their personal problems. They didn't have to sign up for work here. Nobody forced them. He's asking more than standard union rates in the rest of the country."

"It's only a few dollars per man a week, Count Castenelli. We can easily absorb that."

Santiago said. "Sir, with all respect, labor costs are not what are causing our losses. They're being caused by outdated machinery that is so slow in giving us ingots we can ship out that our operation can't keep up with inflation."

"Nor competition, sir. And I can't push our machinery any harder." That was Carter-Wright, whose brow beneath his shock of unruly hair furrowed with worry. "We're already losing valuable hours when we have to stop for repairs, which is far too often. Any serious breakdown with the crusher, for example, which the whole line is dependent on, and it will take months to repair and bring in new parts if necessary and especially a compatible replacement if it came to that."

Changing film, reloading his camera, Jake lost track for a few minutes, and when he once again listening while he shot, he realized that Castenelli had come back to the question of the miners' demand for an increase in pay and was adamant in refusing to hear of it, clearly injecting into a purely business situation such personal disdain of those inferior to him as to override good judgement. The meeting broke up with the Argentines and Carter-Wright barely maintaining a respectful silence when Castenelli's parting remark, as he rose to walk out, was, "I'm not having any illiterate bloody Argie miner tell me or my board of directors how to run a company. Period. I don't want to hear he's still here tomorrow."

There was a long silence after he had closed the door behind him. Pablo Santiago, Carlos Olivares, and Ian Carter-Wright looked at each other mutely until finally Santiago sighed and, shaking his head, rose and left, followed by Olivares.

When they'd gone Gerald broke another silence. "Oh, boy …" and let his breath out in a long low whistle.

"You can say that again, Gerald." Carter-Wright absently snapped a pencil between forefinger and thumb. He rose. "Well, much more of our Count Castenelli and I'll find myself back in England."

"And me in New York," Gerald said.

Jake put away his cameras and went with Carter-Wright and Gerald to lunch.

NINE

—◆—

Rachel Sommerset's home in the South Downs lay a short distance from the little village of Brill-on-Marsh, a cluster of tile-roofed gray-stone houses boasting The Lamb, a pub that had once been a sizeable stable and was the sole social center for much of the area. Close by was a centuries-old Norman church whose surrounding churchyard was filled with the timeworn tombstones and crosses of once village residents who had been fated to stay in the village forever and where, on the walls of the church itself, ivy had grown rampant.

Coming from the village and rounding a sharp bend, one came almost unexpectedly upon Rachel's house itself. Surprisingly little different from others in the village it was two stories and, like the church, was of centuries-weathered gray stone with a tile roof and with small windows that gave it a cottagey aspect. It sat back from the road nestled against a copse of trees and was reached by a flagstone walk flanked on each side by a profusion of flowers. Close by the house there was a vegetable garden in front of a smaller building, once possibly a granary. Now it sheltered some sheep.

Ophelia, a black and white border collie, greeted Rachel as the writer drove up in her Land Rover, a strictly farm vehicle which had seen far better days and which, when the ignition was turned off, always died with short protesting *clunks* from somewhere within its old motor. Rachel got from behind the wheel, wincing slightly from vaguely arthritic knees. "Down, Ophelia. Good girl." And after giving Ophelia a hug, she went up the flagstones to the front door, which was blue and graced with a heavy brass knocker, stopping only to expertly pinch off several dying blooms on one of the walk's flanking rose bushes.

Her hair, gray for some years now, was for the moment windblown and in disarray, and although she was no longer young and slender, it complimented a sense of strength and remaining agility in a figure that, of only medium height, seemed oddly more a workman's than a that of a scholarly intellectual. Getting out her door keys, she eyed a tall ladder that was leaning up against the house, giving access to the roof. Surprisingly and two hours earlier, she had gone up it to affect some minor repairs on a place where the roof had started to leak during a recent rain, and she was still in the overalls she had donned over trousers and a plain cotton shirt. Remembering how winded she'd become climbing while carrying several replacement tiles in a sack slung over her shoulder, and then struggling to replace the tiles that had cracked, she muttered something of a resentful curse at the ladder, "Bloody torture machine. I'm getting too damn old for you."

Quite contrary to the image most of her readers imagined of her and in spite of her fame and her dedication to her work, Rachel lived simply, "uncluttered," she always said, by the impedimenta with which most surrounded themselves. With her love of gardening and the outdoors along with a life habit of frugality rooted in her childhood, she affected many of the minor repairs and upkeep on her property herself. "Gets me free of hard labor nonsense," she always said, referring to the actual business of putting words to paper.

And it did. Rachel did most of her writing in her head and always balked at the business of having actually to write out whatever it was, reluctantly surrendering to the fact that her readers were not mind readers. Some of her most productive literary moments came while, with Ophelia's help, she tended her small flock of sheep, getting them out to pasture in the early morn and then rounding them up at night. Or, as she'd managed yesterday, replacing with strong hands, rough from work, the cracked tiles in her roof that had leaked a recent rain into her bedroom. Far from the mental restriction imposed by her desk, what she would eventually apply to paper would appear spontaneously to be scrawled down in a notebook later or penciled onto lined foolscap and an actually developing manuscript.

Rachel had a PC but its word-processing ability had long since lain idle. She used it only for research. Equally ignoring typewriters, she had always done all her writing with a pencil.

It was a cool day following a stormy one and with often brisk bursts of wind from the north, so the warmth of the interior was welcoming when she entered, closing the door firmly behind her. Years before, when buying the house, she had removed all partitioning on the ground floor so that it now consisted of one spacious whitewashed room where overhead rough-hewn beams held up the floor above. At one end was a small modern kitchen. Rachel was fond of cooking and was a good cook, and she had taken care to outfit the kitchen accordingly with a shamelessly expensive Aga and a stainless-steel refrigerator as well as a dishwasher, and there was good counter space beneath its cabinets.

The room had an almost stark simplicity about it. An open banister stair on a far wall of the room from the kitchen led to the floor above, its entire length flanked by a bookcase filled with those milestones in literature Rachel felt worth always keeping, and here and there among the books were pictures of friends and some of the famed people whose paths she had crossed.

The chimney of the house was dead center of the room along with a fireplace at its base. Before it, Rachel had arranged a couch and several deeply comfortable chairs as well as a low cocktail table on which she kept favored picture or art books which she changed from time to time for new ones that caught her eye at *The Reader*, the book shop at Chichester where she did most of her shopping. There was no other furniture except for a long oaken Jacobean table on four legs for dining along with its high-backed chairs. The flooring was wide-planked, "oak," Rachel always boasted to visitors, with here and there a scattered braided cotton rug.

Rachel put away some groceries she'd bought, made herself a cup of hot chicken broth, and then took it upstairs to a room that was both her bed and work room, one corner of which was partitioned into a room for the rare guest she had stay. Next to it, directly above the kitchen, was the bathroom, which like the kitchen she had modernized so that it had, besides the big tub for occasional soaking, a glass-walled shower. The rest of the room seemed almost barren with its limited furniture and decor. Against the back wall was Rachel's old-fashioned four-poster canopied bed with flanking bedside tables and table lamps, which gave the room a warmth, otherwise missing, and a sense of intimacy. Close by the center-of-the-room chimney, with a second fireplace faced by a deeply comfortable chair and a stand lamp for reading, was where she wrote—a plain heavy wood table, bare except for Rachel's old PC with its monitor and a pencil tray, along with a straight-backed wooden chair with a cushioned seat. Behind the chimney was a file case and some shelving for research books she was reading, some office supplies, and an array of her own published works that from time to time she gifted to close friends.

It was not yet ten in the morning. Rachel was an early riser—she did a great deal of her work before sunrise. She had been up since five and was feeling rather out of sorts, her thoughts in something of a turmoil over her scheduled meeting that day around lunchtime with the American writer who had been thrust on her in some sort of publicity arrangement between the writer's publisher, Crossroads, and her own publisher, the Hanover Group. The prestigious head of Hanover, Sir Ashley Sims-Hanover, was one of her dearest friends. What on earth had dear old Ashely been thinking of? Money, certainly, there was that unattractive side to him. Perhaps boosting American sales or some sort of deal with that unattractive and boring Arson McKain that was strictly publishing and had nothing whatsoever to do with her? Shame on him if that's what it was. He knew how she hated any sort of public exposure. First putting her up for the Nobel, which she'd hardly deserved—she shuddered every time the press still got hold of her with their endlessly inane questions. Now, of all things, he'd arranged for her to commune with an American best-seller with whom she had virtually nothing in common and who wrote almost exclusively for America's horde of romance-starved women. While everything in her bridled at finding herself a pawn in what she saw clearly was a publicity stunt, her thoughts about the woman she was to meet were ambivalent. With time to spare before she had to meet her, she decided to have a bath, a good soak for a few minutes, and have a think. A soak always helped clarify thoughts. Besides, it would help with the arthritis.

First, however, she checked on her phone messages. There were four. Ashley had called about today's meeting with the American and wanting a new photo for the jacket of the fourth printing of *The Spoils of War.* Her old Irish poet friend Emil O'Shaunnesy confirmed he would be delighted to come and stay whenever during the winter—she so loved listening to the ancient Celtic and Gaelic verse he read aloud so beautifully. Thomas Chrichton had called to say he was sending, for her thoughts and critique, his latest essay for *The London Review of Books.* It was on *The Problem of No Such,* William Sconery's controversial foray into existentialist philosophy. And there was the cheerful voice of Daisy McMahon, her far younger second cousin whom she saw as having the most wonderful mind and who was at Oxford reading history. Their most recent exchange of letters had delved deeply into the centuries-old political struggle between church and the power of anointed kings as Western civilization slowly developed.

In the bathroom, she turned on the tub, then, before getting in it, got off her overalls and work clothes and weighed herself. Young Dr. Rice had said she ought to try to lose a kilo or two; she was getting positively thick. And, by golly, she had. She'd lost almost two kilos. Just the same, she avoided her full-length bathroom mirror just as she did whenever possible the one over the sink that had the treacherous habit of pointing out to her wrinkles she preferred not to know about. Getting old was no fun. She was hardly the athletic young sylph who had once helped row Cambridge to victory in the two-woman shell event.

"Age," she muttered. "The curse of womankind."

Before getting into the tub, she took down a large glass container filled with blue crystals, a handful of which she dumped in the water. They'd been recommended as soothing to the nerves by Gilley, the young assistant at the chemist in Chichester.

"Probably just nonsense," Rachel said to herself. "But they turn the water such a lovely blue." Careful not to slip, she got herself slowly over the high edge of the tub and with a sigh of pleasure sank down into it.

TEN

———◆———

"**K**elly Anders," Rachel muttered aloud as she surrendered to the warmth of the bathwater and let her thoughts run free. "Just who are you?"

When first hearing of the meeting she had been forced into, how she had detested Arson McKain. She had also felt intense irritation with Ashley. But true to her early newspaper training and ever curious about everything in writing, especially other writers, she had swallowed her annoyance and had taken time to do some research. She had to know what really went on with the woman who was so distant from her own unique world of letters and exchanges with those serious literary figures who, in their thinking and work, were apostates of public commercialism.

She had skimmed through two of Kelly's books and to her surprise had found her enigmatically interesting. The American, if you ignored her subject matter,

103

turned out to be an especially talented writer, almost a rarity. She was a master of plot and construction and better by far than most in characterization. Even more interestingly, she was clearly capable of great depth of thought. There were hints of it all over both books even if none of that depth ever materialized. Why on earth then had she so limited herself to writing such utterly ridiculous nonsense? Granted she made floods of money. She sold millions of books to millions of romantically starved middle-aged women, fed up with chauvinism in their husbands and everywhere else. But why go on with it? Why whore herself, if she'd once had to, when it was clearly no longer necessary? It didn't make sense.

Photographs showed her to be part of the whole money world. She was not just quite good-looking and dressed as though she'd just done a shoot at *Vogue* magazine; the photos also showed her to have a sensitive face with often an expression of vulnerability. Driven to know more and in spite of herself, Rachel had used her old PC to research Kelly in the archives of various British newspapers—proper ones like the London *Times* as well as some of the luridly sensational rags. She had trawled pages on the kidnaping of the Italian industrialist, Alberto Castenelli, and some of his entourage in Argentina, which had caught world attention with Kelly's finally rescued husband being brought home in a near vegetative state from which he had so far never recovered. Helping magnify the descriptions of the horror that the captives had endured were lurid revelations of his sexual relationship both before and during captivity with a paid companion of Castenelli.

At her friend Ashley's suggestion, Rachel had also secured a video of Kelly's recent TV interview with the famous David Hahn. She didn't believe for a moment all the business of Kelly's losing her father and mother as a child and being raised by an aunt. It was far too glib, as though she had said it before a thousand times. And she'd had the impression that for all his polished skill, Hahn hadn't believed it either. There had been moments when the cameras had also gone in close enough on David Hahn to see that there were questions lurking behind his eyes he'd never asked Kelly and, when close on Kelly, to see she was fearful Hahn might do so.

What Rachel *did* believe was what she saw as the one moment of truth in the interview—Kelly's reason for embarking on a writing career. She had quite plainly stated it was for her the best way to make money, since she'd found she was good at it and that it came relatively easily. There was even more truth in why she wrote for women. She saw them as a far bigger market for her work and thus far more lucrative.

What Kelly hadn't said, however, was why making money was so important, more so than writing better literature when she was clearly capable of it. What she'd seen in the interview, Rachel remembered, both in Hahn's demeanor and Kelly's, told her that for Kelly, money might be the means to an end, but what that end could be, what sort of deep inner need, remained a mystery.

Watching the video, Rachel had found herself becoming more and more intrigued. She'd felt a strange affinity for the woman. Perhaps in person she'd find answers to her curiosity about why such a truly good writer, even a potentially great one, had gone badly the wrong way.

Or, mentally jerking herself back into reality, perhaps not. Their arranged meeting could, and most likely *would*, turn out to be nothing less than a rigidly superficial pretense of a writers' conversation. And it would certainly and most unfortunately be monitored by Arson McKain, a betrayer of true literature if there ever was one, along with that sycophantic horror, Clarissa Chatterly. Both would be bound to hover about like dark vultures.

Besides, when it came to that, what on earth *could* they talk about, herself and this Kelly Anders? They had nothing in common in lifestyle. Kelly, in every aspect, obviously led a life that had to be the exact opposite of her own rapidly getting-elderly self. When they met, she would have to try to look respectable, she thought, so as not to appear too much that way. She'd dress as she did when having to go up to London.

"Curiouser and curiouser," Rachel said aloud, finally getting out of the big bathtub and wrapping herself in a huge warm towel she extracted from a heated towel rack. Why on earth would any woman keep a vegetative and unfaithful husband in such close proximity for years on end? Could she have been still in love with him? Was there some legal reason involved that forced such responsibility on her? Or was it simply a less expensive way to pay for his endless nursing instead of his being put away in a nursing home? She wouldn't know until she met the woman, and even then it might be impossible. Someone who, it seemed, could be keeping some part of herself secret might well balk at divulging anything personal.

Before getting dressed and sallying forth to the dreaded meeting, Rachel made a quick note in a worn old notebook she took from the bookcase flanking the stairs of a thought she'd had earlier that day while up on the roof. After glancing at what she'd scrawled, she returned the notebook, packed with some beginning chapters of her next book and all the thoughts she'd had for months in developing it, to the bookcase and then got dressed in her London clothes, a worn, shamefully old tweed suit supported in appearance by a bright-colored scarf decorated with an antique garnet brooch that had belonged to her grandmother. Her legs encased in the unfamiliarity of stockings, she added a pair of sensible shoes, did the best she could with her hair by getting it back off her face, and after firmly admonishing Ophelia not to follow her, got into her old Land Rover and started it up. She might not be able to match the glamour of the dreaded American, she thought, but at least she would look what others saw as respectable and befitting her age.

On the way to The Lamb, Rachel silently congratulated herself that she'd insisted to Ashley that the American woman come down to Brill-on-Marsh. And to the pub. The lame excuse that she was involved with a sick animal or whatever would have to do. Being on her own turf—she hadn't quite seen having the woman come to her house, hence the bright idea of The Lamb, where Sunday lunches were community affairs and quite wonderful—would unquestionably limit the time of their meeting. It would restrict it, hopefully, to commonplace, impersonal exchanges that would not get her further involved. She could count on the fingers of one hand the people she really enjoyed seeing, talking to, or just plain being with, even if silent. She loathed having so-called friends who, when you got right down to it, were actually no more than acquaintances, casual ships that passed in the night, people with whom your relationship was invariably so meaningless as to be nothing more than a bother and a waste of that most precious aspect of a precariously short life, time.

As a last thought as she approached the pub, she said to herself, "She could, of course, turn out to be a crashing bore. But just the same, Rachel, try to be fair. It's probably not this woman's fault. She's probably been railroaded into meeting you just the way you've been pushed into meeting her, and after all she *is* coming all the way down from London after what must have been an exhausting book tour. So be nice, be welcoming. It will all be over before you know it."

ELEVEN

❖

About an hour out of London on her way to meet Rachel Sommerset, Kelly, who had risen that morning feeling headachy and exhausted, had a dismal feeling that she was coming down with something. "Of all times," she thought. She managed to lift her attention from her iPad and look out the window of the limo at the passing countryside. It had changed. London, its traffic-jammed exits, then suburbia with its often dreary and unimaginative architecture and clutter, had given way to a verdant and open countryside of rolling hills with only the occasional little village tucked away in an unexpected valley and where large flocks of sheep roamed vast green pastures separated here and there by small copses of trees and occasional hedgerows.

In spite of a somber sunless sky, she felt drawn to it in its unfamiliarity as though into a painting, and she suddenly had an intense feeling that she wanted to be alone with what she saw and not be stuck in the limo with Clarissa Chatterley and Arson McKain. Their ceaseless chatter was becoming more and more invasive. As long as she had to face the dreaded Sommerset woman she'd prefer to do it her way, on her own terms, and not have her publisher escort hanging on every word, but she had failed miserably in a tactful effort to leave them behind. "I'll be fine on my own, really. Save you the trouble."

"No trouble at all." That was Clarissa Chatterly, not about to be suppressed. "I love the South Downs. And I know the pub we're meeting her at. The Lamb. Lovely place. The local diner, or if you wish, MacDonald's." She laughed at her comparison. "Well, not quite that. Just the only decent place to eat for miles. All the gentry go there Sundays, mix it up with the sheep farmers. Very democratic."

"I heard they're famous for their steak and kidney pies," Arson offered.

Clarissa laughed. "Given this is important sheep country, it should be *lamb* and kidney, but I'll pass on it and settle for champagne. Two of our most important writers meeting? Doesn't happen every day."

Kelly managed a smile but it made her cringe inwardly. She had a feeling Clarissa didn't mean a word of what she said.

They were on a main highway and, suddenly branching off onto a small local road, they dipped down from the crest of one of the rolling hills into a wide expanse of verdant openness where it seemed to Kelly there were more grazing sheep than ever. The road became rough graded dirt, and they headed toward a village stretched out against a low wooded rise. The limo's jarring over pot holes made Kelly more and more aware of her headache, and she again inwardly cursed that of all days she had to be feeling rotten and not on top of the world.

The Lamb, an oddly long, rectangular, one-story stone building, gray with age and partially covered with ivy, had been converted, Clarissa said, from what had once been an exchange stable. "The post came through here back in Victoria's day and before, and this was where they housed fresh teams of horses." It sat back a few yards from the road entering the village, and the half-grass, half-gravelly space before it was packed with cars, many of them well-worn Land Rovers and other farm vehicles.

Getting out of the limo with the others, Kelly suddenly felt giddy. The cars in the parking lot and the building that was the pub swam in front of her. "Been sitting too long," she thought. She drew a deep breath and felt her heart beating rapidly. "Oh, God, this is it. Rachel Sommerset. And no escape." She was hit by a stab of anxiety she hadn't felt since school years and facing the principal for some infringement of discipline. At the same time she wondered why she should feel any anxiety at all and firmly resolved to get a grip on herself. With a stream of best-sellers behind her, why should she feel anxious about meeting *any* other author, even such an apparently famed and well respected one? She felt another wave of giddiness. Steadying herself and trying not to be noticed, she stood a moment, finding unexpected relief in fixating on the pub sign, the wooly dark-faced head of a lamb, hanging over the door above with a sub sign dangling from it that said "The Lamb." And then, since she realized that just standing there might look peculiar, she summoned sudden strength and joined McKain and Chatterly in entering the pub.

Inside, she was assailed by deafening noise and confusion. The place was packed. Men and women in informal country attire or farm work clothes lined the bar where they were served by the publican, a balding giant in a bright red apron, the sleeves of his wide striped shirt rolled up above the elbows. His hands full with orders, he was being helped by his wife, a dumpy, rotund little woman with puffy white hair and a ruddy face. Some customers were watching a football match on the TV that hung on the wall at the bar's end, volume turned high. Others, an equal mix of farmers and gentry, were milling about, drinks in hand, chatting or greeting friends and neighbors or table-hopping among a dozen neatly set blue-clothed dining tables, all of them well occupied and served by two pretty young women with trays and white aprons.

Kelly, trying to focus on it all, felt badly overdressed in her smart designer suit with accompanying jewelry, her high heels, Hermès scarf, and her flawless makeup and hair styling. Again everything swam dizzily in front of her, and when she fought the giddiness down, she became aware that Clarissa Chatterly had firmly linked arms with her and that she was being propelled forward with Clarissa, slightly myopic, having difficulty spotting someone.

"Ah," Kelly suddenly heard McKain exclaim and Clarissa follow with "Miss Sommerset, there you are. We finally made it." And standing against an empty chair pushed in against the table, Kelly found her eyes fixed on the famed British author, seated with a glass of wine across the table. There was a brief moment when she was only aware of hazel eyes, rather disordered gray hair that was partially held back with combs, and a weather-seamed face which was approaching elderly. And then the woman rose and was pushing her away through people and around the table, and Kelly saw she was short, no longer slender, and dressed in a faded old tweed suit with a bright scarf tucked in around her neck with some sort of antique brooch holding it in place.

For an instant she thought she had to be mistaken. Who was this woman? Surely not the famous writer she had come to meet. She hardly looked the scholarly intellectual she'd expected. Then the woman was there, warmly grasping both her hands and saying, "Kelly! How awfully sweet of you to come all the way down here. I so appreciate it. And do sit down, my dear. Are you all right? You look quite exhausted. Here, Arson," commandingly, "be useful. Set this chair straight." And Kelly found herself suddenly seated with

Rachel Sommerset right next to her. Still firmly holding both her hands in hers, she was saying in a cultivated Cambridge accent that seemed strangely at odds with her appearance, "I've heard so much about you and have so looked forward to meeting you. Arson, get Kelly a drink. What you will have, my dear? I'm well into some Pinot Noir. Tommy, he's our publican, keeps an excellent cellar."

Kelly slowly came to her senses and realized that she was staring idiotically at the woman's face in which then, and to her surprise, she suddenly saw intense intelligence.

After that, the rest was a blur. While luncheon was being served and eaten and the wine decanter frequently passed around, Kelly, fighting now ferocious pain in her head and waves of giddiness again, found herself not in charge with diffident yet commanding control as she had planned or putting on a make-believe delight at being there. Unusually on the defensive, she found herself answering a barrage of questions about her trip over from the States and her book tour (real sympathy there) and feeling relieved whenever Clarissa's or Arson's promotional talk that was embarrassingly out of place was mercifully interrupted by some neighbor or workman stopping by to have a word with Rachel, with whom they seemed astonishingly familiar and at ease for all her fame.

From a burly sheep farmer: "Did you get that patch put on the roof, Rachel?"

"I did indeed, Michael, and I'll return your ladder

tomorrow. Meet friends from London down to ogle the natives. Kelly, my good friend and savior, Michael Potter, a wizard on roof repair."

Michael gave a passing friendly nod and then said, "Keep the damned ladder a while, luv. Make sure the patch holds. If it doesn't, I'll pop over some time and lend a hand."

A busty young woman in overalls passed, dangling on the arm of a redheaded young man with a punk hairdo and whose T-shirt screamed "World's Fair 1939." "Rachel, can I come over and borrow that cookbook we talked about? The one with the prune cake mix?"

"Of course, darling. Late in the day is best when I'm not trying to write some damn thing or other."

Whatever she'd been expecting, Kelly thought at that moment, the meeting she'd imagined with Rachel Sommerset wasn't anything like any of this, and Rachel Sommerset herself not this welcoming woman who seemed everyone's friend and who, except for her Cambridge speech, was hardly what she'd imagined the great writer to be.

Lunch over, when the plan had been to head straight back to London, Kelly found herself getting no support for it from either Arson McKain or Clarissa when Rachel surprisingly insisted they drop by her place for coffee first. "You simply must see her house, Kelly," Clarissa burbled. "It's absolutely divine."

Kelly had begun to feel quite ill. Her head pounded worse than ever, and she fought off waves of nausea.

She wanted desperately to simply slouch in the seat of the limousine and go to sleep. But that would be embarrassing professionally as well as socially, and as though in a confused dream, as though she were someone else and not herself, she found herself swept along, unprotesting.

Getting in and out of the limo and driving the short distance to Rachel's house was agony. Twice Kelly felt herself black out. When finally arriving, it took an effort to return the greeting of Ophelia, Rachel's friendly border collie, who leapt all over everybody, especially Arson, who didn't much like dogs, or to express appreciation of the richly tended flower garden that, along with a vegetable patch, flanked the flagstones to the door. And then Kelly found herself seated in a deeply comfortable lounge chair in a very large whitewashed room and before a fireplace in which there were still the glowing embers of fire. "Plunk ye down, everyone," Rachel said. "I'll get coffee. Or does anybody want what to me has always been the curse of England—tea?"

Coffee won favor. "Arson, inspire the fire to life, please. Wood's right in that old box over there," And Rachel hustled off to the kitchen, leaving Arson McKain to tend to the fire and Clarissa Chatterly and Kelly to themselves and in a silence which was broken only once or twice by Clarissa with a flattering remark about the "gorgeous big room."

Kelly welcomed the lack of talk. She had begun to feel terribly cold. She was almost shaking with it, and everything, the room, Arson, Clarissa, suddenly seemed far away as though seen through the wrong end of a telescope. Their voices and Rachel's when she returned were distant and almost echoing like voices far down a tunnel. She made an effort and tried to focus and take charge, but couldn't. Everything around her seemed to slip farther and farther away.

Then Rachel was offering her a coffee cup and asking if she wanted sugar, but when Kelly tried to sit up straight and take the cup she found herself looking not at Rachel but at the smiling face of a very young man in a white shirt with a bow tie and wearing a denim jacket. He had a stethoscope hanging around his neck and glanced at a thermometer he pulled from under one of her arms. She realized she was lying, heavily covered with blankets, in a narrow bed in small whitewashed room, looking through a door at a much larger space like the one in which she'd been waiting for coffee. There were curtains on a small window, and a bedside table with a lamp, and some country prints on one wall, and Rachel Sommerset was sitting on a stiff-backed cane chair next to her, staring at her with a half-smile, her expression anxious.

She tried to sit up and was gently eased back down by the young man. There were oxygen lines going into her nostrils and an IV line in one arm.

"Don't try to get up," he said. "Not yet. I'm giving you bottled fresh air for today and maybe tomorrow. And a saline solution. You were pretty dehydrated." He turned to Rachel, "Her temperature has come right down."

Rachel said, "You've been very sick, Kelly. We thought hospital, except it's quite a ways off and Dr. Rice and I decided it better to have you here with me. Just try to rest. Dr. Rice doesn't want you to do anything right now except sleep."

"You got hit with a double whammy, young lady." The doctor stuffed his stethoscope into his jacket pocket. "Flu and pneumonia both. Seen it happen before. One moment you are up. The next, down all the way. You had a temperature of 105 all day yesterday. It's coming on to fairly normal now. I've got you on antibiotics. Old-fashioned penicillin, actually, for pneumonia."

Kelly managed to find her voice. Her tongue felt like lead. "Arson?"

"I packed him and Clarissa off to London," Rachel said. She laughed. "They were just getting in the way. I'm going to call him now and tell him we think you are out of the woods. Meanwhile, you're not to worry about a thing. Just sleep. I'll bring you up some chicken broth in a while."

She rested one of her hands reassuringly on one of Kelly's an instant then rose and headed for the stairs with the young doctor. Kelly heard their murmuring voices distantly as they went down and then felt herself drifting off to sleep. What had happened? Why was she there? She'd come out of London to meet the dreaded Rachel Sommerset and had met her and hadn't gone back. Instead, she was lying in a bed. Where? In Rachel's house? And sick. She couldn't grasp it. It didn't make any sense, none of it did. Struggling to understand, her thoughts slowly drifted into nothingness.

—➤ ◄—

On their way back to London in the limo, Arson McKain and Clarissa Chatterly were relatively silent, each reflecting on the jolting occurrence that had so unexpectedly happened and sent them back without Kelly. On his part McKain saw a positive result from it. The meeting he had so arduously persuaded Rachel's publisher to set up had perhaps cost him dearly in any returned favors. He had been merciless in almost forcing Hanover Publishing to cooperate and had only succeeded by burning some business bridges he would have preferred to keep intact. The meeting had succeeded beyond his expectations, however. First, Rachel Sommerset seemed to take to Kelly Anders almost immediately, even though Kelly, beginning with the drive from London, had been strangely silent and withdrawn—possibly not feeling well, he had thought at the time. Then, after the first shock of her becoming ill and thoroughly annoyed at Rachel Sommerset's insistence that she take her in charge, he began to see a plus side to it in spite of all the inconvenience and anxiety for Kelly's welfare. The first day back in his office, he'd be in touch with the right people in the right newspapers. He could almost write the leads himself—"Nobel winner nurses stricken

American." It would elevate Crossroads Publishing's image and sales almost everywhere.

◆➤◆

An equally silent Clarissa tried to hold down a mounting sense of bitter jealousy and disappointment. She had been badly taken back by Rachel Sommerset's warm welcome in which, quite amazingly, the author had actually seemed to like Kelly. It defied understanding. The two were miles apart. Kelly might indeed be a best-selling author where American women were concerned, but Sommerset was renowned worldwide and considered a national treasure by the English. And then, of all things, Sommerset had taken charge of everything and not packed Kelly off to a hospital when she fell ill. It wasn't fair, Clarissa thought. It had left her out in the cold and cost her the prestige and authority she'd hoped to gain by being basically in charge of the meeting.

In the darkest corner of her heart, she had nothing but ill thoughts about both women, especially Sommerset.

TWELVE

❖

Rachel was almost surprised at her first reaction to Kelly's being taken unexpectedly ill. After the alarm that she would have felt for anyone passing out in her house, or anywhere else for that matter, and almost without thinking of any consequences, practicality took over. Until they knew exactly what had stricken Kelly, she thought an immediate rush to the hospital was not only difficult and time consuming, but possibly dangerous. She had complete faith in young Dr. Rice, who happened to be close by at The Lamb and who appeared within minutes after Clarissa was dispatched to alert him. He was quite firm in agreeing that any move to the local hospital could be unnecessarily risky.

"She'll be better off right where she is," he'd said. Within minutes after he helped Arson McKain and herself get Kelly upstairs and into the guest room bed, he had produced an IV bottle and line along with a bottle of oxygen from the trunk of his car as well as the necessary antibiotic. "Goes with being a country GP," he'd said to McKain. "You have to be prepared for almost anything that's not in your office. Got stuck with an amputation once out in a hay field. And as for deliveries ..." He laughed.

Once Kelly was put on oxygen and an IV line run, Rachel was confronted with the problem of McKain and Chatterly, who stood about offering unnecessary and unwanted advice on nearly everything until their presence became unbearable. They had to go. Getting rid of them proved awkward, however, and there were moments when Rachel was convinced their concern for Kelly had more to do with Kelly as a commercial proposition than for the woman herself. It was finally only due to young Dr. Rice that she was able to prevail without harsh words and possibly bad feeling that would end up in Ashley Sims-Hanover's lap, and she didn't want that.

They had finally gone in time to make late dinner in London and she and Dr. Rice were having coffee when she suddenly realized, and again to her surprise, that she rather welcomed Kelly's unexpected presence. Arranging for the district nurse, looking after her with meals, and fetching medicine from the pharmacy in Chichester were a distraction from work and that she had to admit to herself was a welcomed one. She had become desperately frustrated in trying to get her new novel up and running. Her thoughts were piling up, her notes along with them, and nothing seemed to resolve itself. She probably never should have embarked on anything new so soon after *The Spoils of War*, which in a way had quite worn her out. Probably the only person other than herself who realized the cost of five years of nonstop writing, writing, writing, whether in her head, in notes, or actually in a manuscript, was dear old Ashley. And in fact, without his guidance and encouragement, she never would have come near to finishing the epic.

"He should have been given the Nobel, not me," she often said. There had been moments when she wondered not only why she had ever undertaken such a project, but why, in the first place, she had ever taken up writing novels. Nothing about it was easy. She had been scribbling an essay for an unimportant and effete literary periodical shortly after Cambridge when she had begun to see authoring a novel as something beyond any ordinary writing. It had seemed the literary Everest to be climbed, and if you didn't successfully reach the summit, you were of no great importance in the world of literature. In reading all the great classics, she had seen novelists not just as one kind of writer among many but as people with an ability and talent beyond the reach of people like herself.

Then why had she tried to do it? Recklessness? An egotistical desire to be above the crowd? Certainly it was with no idea of making money because novels paid little when she had started. But she had embarked on doing it, regardless, naively not realizing what she was in for and defiantly and with a pretended confidence when actually propelled, probably, by some sort of crazy motivation simply to be on top looking down and not on the bottom gazing ever upward in envy and awe.

With a strange sense of unease that had never left her, she remembered her struggle with the first one, and vaguely one horrible week while writing it when she had discovered a major redundancy in a critically important section. The redundancy had reflected on a dozen other parts of the book, like the ripples in a quiet pool of water if a stone were dropped into it. It had left her not just frustrated but badly frightened, and it had taken weeks to rectify and set straight while all the time anxious that she wasn't doing the corrections correctly.

She had persisted, however, and eventually had submitted her handwritten effort to half a dozen publishers at once. Several rejected her politely, telling her to keep trying, they'd like to see her next effort. Another laughingly told her to learn to use a typewriter as handwritten novels went out with the quill pen. But to her astonishment she received an acceptance by the prestigious Hanover Group and, even more astonishing, with a request from its head, the then far younger but already renowned Sir Ashley Sims-Hanover, to come and see him personally.

"You're a writer, girl," she remembered him saying. "A writer among few, and I want to spend some time with you to help you get this novel as straight as we both think it should and can be before we send it out to the bookshops." She'd then found herself spending hours with him going over one thing after another where she hadn't been clear, been careless or contradictory, but more often where she simply had not realized the potential of her own idea.

Due to his extraordinary support, the success of that first effort had, when she read the reviews, seemed almost ordained and commonplace, and without trepidation she'd embarked on another and then a third. In complete confidence now, of course, yet always when it came to the actual writing, she'd be beset, day and night, as to whether things were going right or not. There was always a constant rereading, revising, rewriting. Sometimes she would find herself, never quite satisfied, going over a single sentence a dozen times, seeking just the right word for something that would make a world of difference in the sentence's meaning. She haunted both dictionary and thesaurus.

And always, no matter the tremendous success of everything she wrote, there was always the nagging feeling that she could have done it better somehow.

All that was true when it came to *The Spoils of War.* The work, the anxiety, the absolute endlessness of it until it was finished had exhausted her. It was almost with distaste that she now thought of her current work, which had so excited her when she'd first had the idea for it. It needed to be put aside for a while until she could get herself back together again.

The American writer, she thought, had come to visit

at just the right time. She lived in a different world, she wrote for different readers, but she was a writer, nevertheless, and a proven good one. It would be fun to determine what she did or didn't suffer when putting pen to paper.

THIRTEEN

—◆—

Jake came out of a sound sleep to find himself in what seemed at first a blaze of light but which he quickly realized were the room lights. He was adding up that he was in a Quonset hut at the Argoronorte mine and wondering why the lights had come on when he saw that he wasn't alone. There were two men in work clothes standing over his bed. Miners? One had an ugly automatic hand gun pointed right in his face. The other, a machete slung loosely over his shoulder, had a length of duct tape stretched between his two hands, and before Jake had a chance to react, the tape was slapped across his mouth, he was yanked forward, and it was secured behind his head.

"No word," the man hissed. His Spanish accent was strong. "No word." When he slapped Jake's face, twice and hard, rocking Jake over on one side, Jake felt a rise of terror through his whole system. Who were these guys? What was happening? There was no chance to think further. He was hauled to his feet, seized by the scruff of his neck, his head pushed down and with no clothing except the boxer shorts he slept in, he was propelled from the room.

Outside the Quonset hut he found himself pushed up against Gerald, flanked by two other men, his mouth also sealed with duct tape and his hands taped behind his back. Gerald had on nothing but a T-shirt, and his eyes were wide with bewilderment and fear.

Jake took another blow to the head and then, head forced down again, was marched with Gerald away from the row of night-lit Quonset huts on a long dark walk past all the night-silent buildings that housed the massive gold extracting machinery. It seemed forever until he found himself at the foot of the ladder stairs leading up to the yawning mouth of the mine. Now shaking with the night cold, his bare feet hurting badly, he was struck again, viciously kicked and forced upward until he reached the wide rock shelf where the motionless backhoe stood mutely awaiting dawn's first shift.

Left standing on his own for a brief moment, he vaguely saw in the darkness two more men as they came close. Both were armed with automatic rifles. Then he was seized and lifted and slung like a sack onto the rocks loaded on one of the half-filled rail cars, rolling up against Gerald, already there.

There was a murmur of voices, arguing. The train's motor whined and it moved forward into the mine.

After a while it stopped. There was more arguing, louder now, and the rail car jerked and swayed slightly, and Jake realized that they had branched off into one of the lesser tunnels of the mine leading away from the main one. He thought for a moment to roll off the car, take the blow of landing—unlike Gerald, his hands weren't tied behind his back—but a sense that there was no space between the car and the tunnel wall stopped him. He'd be crushed.

The train had gone what he felt was a long way when it ground to a stop. Lights flared—the head lamps of several miners. Heaved off the rocks of the rail car and onto his feet, Jake saw to his horror that he and Gerald weren't the only ones. Trapped in the oval glare of head lamps was Alberto Castenelli, clad in the bottom half only of his silk pajamas, his hands taped behind him and tape wrapped across his mouth. Next to him in a nightgown was a terrified Teresa, made equally helpless with duct tape.

One of the captors pushed up against the Italian and Jake recognized the short, stocky Pulmumarca. The miner cursed Castenelli in a volley of Spanish and slapped his face, left and right, hard, then kneed him in the groin, and when Castenelli doubled over in agony, butted his face with his knee. Castenelli fell, writhing in pain, his screaming muffled, and was hauled to his feet and marched up through a narrow gap in the side of the tunnel wall where there were crude steps chiseled into the rock. Teresa was shoved along behind him and Gerald and Jake next, stumbling, torn, and with their bleeding feet searching the crude steps and trying not to fall.

The climb was forever. At times it was on their hands and knees when it was only crawl space or prodded on with rifle butts when having to slither and squeeze sideways where the crevasse in the rock narrowed to body width. When they finally came to the climb's end, it was into icy air and the rough, boulder-strewn, harsh surface of the Andean foothills where occasional scattered growth of coarse mountainous shrubs and grasses tore at them. They were forced endlessly upward on a steep slope, sometimes upright and stumbling, sometimes on their hands and knees. The sky was beginning to lighten when the low feathered branch of a wind-stunted tree blocking their way was pushed aside to reveal a hole in the rocks only large enough to crawl through, and Jake, along with Castenelli, Teresa, and Gerald, found himself roughly forced into a small low-ceilinged cave.

There was a volley of harsh angry Spanish. Teresa had her face slapped and, duct tape removed, managed to translate. "We're to stay right here until we pay five million dollars. They will tell us how tomorrow. If we try to escape or cry out, we will be shot. They will give us some blankets and food and water later today."

There was another volley of Spanish. Her face was slapped again, hard. The tape was removed from her hands and then all the tape from Castenelli and from Gerald and Jake, too. The headlamps of the several miners who had brought them winked out, their captors moved cautiously away from the cave, and they were alone in the breaking dawn with Castenelli's whimpering and Teresa's sobbing. And with Gerald cursing under his breath.

FOURTEEN

Kelly's recovery was slow. Mrs. Hedges, a health services nurse, came once a day for the first week to check her progress, help her to the bathroom she was too weak to make on her own, and, after several days, help her bathe in the huge old-fashioned tub on legs, in which Rachel had indulged herself, in the otherwise modern bathroom. She remained in the bed in the little guest room, and Rachel cooked her meals and in the evenings brought in a portable TV that they looked at together.

Embarrassment at her sudden illness, and her helplessness because of it, didn't leave Kelly easily. At first simply astonished at finding herself literally in the hands of the woman she'd dreaded meeting and even worse had scorned, she began bit by bit to see Rachel in a light other than her being a famous author. As it became clear to her that Rachel quite truly didn't regard her sudden presence as any sort of a serious problem, she started, to her surprise, to see Rachel as a warm and friendly person and to accept her unconventional and often abrupt way of coping with any problem that arose. Going to bed one night and chatting with Rachel, who insisted she keep the door closed once they slept "so you won't have to listen to me snore," Kelly suddenly felt a rush of warm friendly feeling for her.

From then on, resigning herself to being looked after and to not being back in New York, where Arson McKain had taken charge of all her affairs, including Gerald, she no longer felt awkward. The older woman, most of the time in workman's clothes and a heavy sweater, became a familiar and welcome sight whenever she appeared.

On the first day that Kelly was able to come downstairs, carried down by a smiling Michael Potter, Rachel's sheep farmer friend who had dropped by to help with some drain repairs, and when she went to help Rachel peel potatoes in the kitchen, she was suddenly filled with chagrin at how aggressively dismissive she had planned to be when told she had to meet her. She had come there to disdain, to deprecate their meeting as much as possible and to regard the famed Nobel writer as a complete equal, if indeed not a lesser success than herself. Now she thought, how could she possibly have felt that way? All that turbulent, angry emotion had gone, to be replaced with not just a kind of wonderment but with a growing sense of comforting security at being in Rachel's house. More and more she had a feeling that she had always been there, and Rachel herself seemed as familiar as though she had known her forever. Impossible, but there it was.

With that was a growing curiosity about Rachel's writing. Except for once when she'd awoken very early and in the half light of dawn had seen Rachel scratching something in a small leather notebook, Kelly hadn't seen or heard her write a word, not even once. The table the other side of the fireplace from her bed where she said she did her writing remained neatly bare except for the notebook, the old PC and its monitor, which Rachel called "Wiki," and said she used only for research, two lined pads of foolscap, a narrow tray filled, surprisingly, with pencils and the leather notebook she'd seen Rachel writing in.

It seemed to Kelly that Rachel did everything *but* write. She was forever tending to her small flock of sheep, feeding her chickens or slaughtering one and plucking all its feathers for a next-day roast, or was off someplace on errands in her beat-up old Land Rover, Ophelia sitting possessively on the passenger seat. Or she was back up on the roof once again "trying to make the damn patch work" and furious that even though she'd spent precarious hours at it, drips of water still found their way through, regardless, whenever it rained.

Kelly had been there slightly more than a week and Rachel was off someplace when curiosity got the better of her. She struggled up out of the deeply comfortable lounge chair Rachel had picked up for her at a thrift shop in Chichester, a sizeable town ten miles away, and where Rachel said you could find a million good things at rock-bottom prices. "Five quid for this thing, love," she said after somehow heaving the heavy chair up the stairs herself and placing it before the fire place.

Kelly, still a little unsteady on her feet, went around to the table-desk and stood a while looking down at it. This barren spot was where Rachel had won the Man Booker award, where she had written *The Spoils of War*, said by all to be an extraordinary and profoundly perspective work. It chronicled the enormous change in all of British society during and after World War One, when centuries old ways of life in the West had come to a shatteringly abrupt end. Its principal body, the critics said, was delving deep into the slow dissolution of a solid, long-titled British family under the pressure of the war's many terrifying aspects and its economic class–destroying aftermath. Seen through an intimate history of the sizeable family of the great British banker, Lord Galbraith, owner of vast estates and a stately home on the South Downs as well, it chronicled the downfall of the family as well as the extraordinary change in circumstances of all his friends, business associates, and various estate employees. Woven through it, as though a chain holding together its many disparate sections, were two heartbreakingly beautiful love stories that filmmakers were rabid to exploit.

"It's fiction, of course," Rachel said when it was published. She shrugged off, as quite normal, that the finely detailed lives and fortunes, the hopes and dreams and tragedies of three generations of some several hundred people were all the product of one woman's mind. "Nobody in it actually exists."

Where on earth was it, Kelly wondered. She hadn't seen it downstairs when she'd come in the week before, nor upstairs any place. There had to be a copy someplace. Probably tucked modestly away in one of the bookcases lining the stairway, she thought. Typical of Rachel. Her eye fell on the leather notebook she'd seen Rachel scratching in that lay on her table desk. She opened it carefully. It seemed to be a diary, in part at least. An entry on an otherwise empty page and written in Rachel's small neat hand said, "Poor Kelly taken ill. Keeping her here." She turned back several pages. "Kelly Anders visit in two days. Scares me to death. Huge success in States. Pics show her all high-fashion and super confident. Has sold piles of books." And on another page, "K day tomorrow. Think meet at pub is safest."

Had Rachel conceivably been nervous about meeting her? Kelly flipped a few more pages. On one, written the week before she'd come, she read, "Just can't see Bryan yet. Who is he, what *is* his stupid hang-up in life. Opening chapters and he seems too much a Thomas Hardy character. And his circumstances are too bland."

How like the problem she'd run into with Marcus on her flight over. Kelly smiled and vaguely remembered her struggle with Marcus having ideas of his own that weren't his author's. She read on. "Have a big rethink, Rachel. Stop procrastinating and get this damned book off the ground. Been making notes far too long, volumes of them, almost a book in themselves (maybe just publish them the way they are instead—joke). You'll be dead and buried before you ever write it all up at this rate."

Rachel's notes had to be thoughts on her current or next novel, Kelly realized, and clearly writing wasn't all that easy for Rachel. Also clearly, if she'd started the actual writing of the novel, she wasn't anywhere near finished with it. Kelly flipped pages of the notebook. Except for the several pages she'd looked at, it was empty—not a word. But surely she must have made more notes someplace. Arson had said that she'd been plotting her next novel for several years. Perhaps she put them somewhere else?

She started to put the notebook neatly back on the exact spot she'd found it and had turned to go back to the lounge chair when she saw the small tidy tier of shelves under one side of the desk, up against the chimney and almost out of sight.

On one shelf there was a mountainous pile of lined yellow foolscap. She knelt and carefully took out the top hundred pages or so held together with a big clip. It was indeed a manuscript, carefully written in pencil in Rachel's small neat hand, three hundred–odd words at least to a page, its title *The Spoils of War*, and Kelly realized it was a draft of Rachel's famous masterwork.

FIFTEEN

◆

Holding the stack of foolscap, she could not bring herself to believe that this was indeed the famous book. A whole, huge novel written by hand and in pencil? The revelation nearly obliterated any other thought in Kelly. For what seemed forever, she stared at the opening page filled with its minutely neat scrawl and then glanced up at the silent dark face of the PC's monitor. Remembering Rachel saying to someone that she only used a computer for research, the monitor's presence suddenly seemed a silent rebuff at its enforced neglect.

Kelly shifted her eyes from the manuscript's title and read its well-known opening sentences. "Permanency is never long permanent. So thought Lady Patricia Hendricks, invited to tea by Lady Galbraith, and as she came up the long tree- and shrubbery-lined drive in her four-in-hand carriage, her coachman cracking his whip to urge the horses on, her life-tired elderly eyes regarded with no small amount of resentment the approaching stateliness of the great Galbraith Hall. 'You'll crumble, yes you will,' she thought. 'Like everything else in this world.' It was nineteen fourteen, the Archduke of Austria had just been assassinated...."

Kelly read on. First hesitantly and then page after page until she finished the thick clip of foolscap. Drawn completely into what she had read, she put it away and had taken up another thick clip of pages, one of a dozen more, when she heard the clunky, piston-knocking sound of Rachel's Land Rover arriving. Any more reading would have to wait. She quickly put back the second big clip of papers and, her search for another notebook forgotten, returned to the lounge chair.

When Rachel came up the stairs, followed by Ophelia, she at first thought Kelly asleep, but then Kelly opened her eyes and said, "Hi."

"Hi. Are you alright?"

"Fine. Just dozing. Where did you go?" Kelly put her arms around Ophelia, who jumped onto her lap as though Kelly had always lived there, and Kelly briefly thought of Mischief and missed her.

"Chichester. Hardware store. A few things needed in the workshop. Nails and screws and a new hinge for the chicken roost door. Plus a few odds and ends for the kitchen. Ready for dinner? It's gone past six."

"Sure."

Rachel went downstairs to cook and Kelly, while she was gone and before she came upstairs with a tray of delicious roast chicken and sautéed fresh vegetables from the garden, thought about her book. She'd never read writing like it anywhere. The people in it were so terribly alive in all their complexities and so very different from each other, the scenic descriptions so vivid they were like looking at a Turner or Constable. She couldn't wait to read on and felt frustrated that she couldn't right then. Maybe Rachel would drive off tomorrow on some more errands. The critics were right. Just as everyone said, the book was like Tolstoy. It had that kind of amazing depth. Every word brought you deep down into it.

Rachel brought up a tray of her own, too, and first they chatted a bit, with Rachel telling Kelly all the local gossip, and then they ate, mostly in silence, until Rachel said, "Kelly, do think you feel up to driving out a bit tomorrow? The weather is supposed to be quite lovely. Like today. I have to go to Miss Tiggy's, bring her a pie or something. She's not far and it's a nice drive."

"Who is Miss Tiggy?" Kelly smiled at the name.

"Miss Tiggy Winkle, the little hedgehog laundress? Beatrix Potter's wonderful creation, remember?"

"Oh, yes," but Kelly didn't. She'd known nothing of Beatrix Potter in her childhood. There'd been no books, no reading, except she vaguely remembered some story called *Peter Rabbit* she'd once heard some kids talking about.

"Her name's Brewster or something like that. I never did get it straight. I call her Miss Tiggy Winkle because she takes in laundry for some of the farm workers around here who don't have wives to do it for them. She's a wonderful little thing. Looks like a hedgehog, just like Potter's Miss Tiggy Winkle."

Miss Tiggy sounded intriguing to Kelly. Even better would be to go for a drive with Rachel through what she remembered vaguely as the beauty of the South Downs. "Oh, yes. I'd love to go," she said. "Sounds like fun. And I feel quite up to it."

And did. Further reading of Rachel's extraordinary work would have to wait another unbearable day of frustration until she could read on.

❧❧

Feeling pleased at Kelly's progress, Rachel's thoughts went back to first meeting her. She had been more than pleasantly surprised when Kelly had been escorted into the crowded and noisy pub by the two publishers. The strange affinity she had felt for her when viewing the Hahn interview had intensified. It was as though she had always known the American. And she had felt an immediate concern for Kelly, who had looked pale and exhausted and slightly bewildered. Rachel's own natural instincts of protectiveness rose at once—she wondered if Kelly wasn't ill. It made her feel a definite need to make the meeting, as she had promised herself, friendly and uncomplicated by the promotional zeal of Kelly's two escorts. It was the basic reason why she had insisted they return to her home to talk. She'd thought The Lamb an ideal place to escape Kelly, except for polite formalities, if Kelly turned out to be a horror, but this had not been the case.

Kelly's passing out, a thunderbolt of sorts and at the moment quite frightening, had caught everyone off guard. When young Dr. Rice had said that it would be preferable if Kelly were left in her bed upstairs, as long as she was carefully looked after, Rachel had seen an ideal chance to get to know the woman and to have at least some of her curiosity satisfied. Perhaps less of a surprise because it happened so naturally, she quickly found herself genuinely liking her, which made having her so much easier than she'd ever expected.

There was so much about Kelly, she kept thinking, that the Hahn interview hadn't told her.

SIXTEEN

❖

Miss Tiggy was everything Rachel had described. She really did look like a hedgehog, Kelly thought. She was short and dumpy, wore carpet slippers and a white apron over a very old wool dress that was clearly patched here and there, and she had little brown eyes each side of a sharp little nose and a shock of very short hair, some of which was in paper curlers and stood straight up from her head, making her look decidedly prickly and hedgehog-ish. Laundry lines on poles were hung generously with fresh washed sheets, trousers, men's long underwear, and socks, all drying in the sun before her little one-story brick house which, as dumpy as Miss Tiggy herself, had a thatched roof and was on the fringe of another village a quarter hour's drive from Brill-on-Marsh.

Rachel had brought an apple pie she'd baked herself with apples from one of her own apple trees, and nothing would do for Miss Tiggy but that she share it with her visitors. She laid a clean white cloth across the table in her little kitchen where an old coal range heated the kettle and served up tea in odd-size cracked and chipped old cups along with generous slices of the pie.

She and Rachel talked endlessly about local affairs and people: who had just got married, or died, who had a brand new member in their household or who was rebuilding their house or had bought a new car or had recently taken sick, and who had found enough money to go on vacation, of all things. Feeling a little out of it, Kelly went to look at Miss Tiggy's flower garden behind the house that began just beyond two wide, worn stone steps leading down from the back door. She had hardly been confronted by the jumble of color in iris and phlox, lupins and foxgloves, and a gorgeous array of some violet border flowers when her breath caught and her hand went to her mouth to stifle a cry. In the middle of it all there was a stunted little crab apple tree.

Kelly sat down slowly on the stone, overcome by a sudden wave of emotion that was a dark, heavy weight in her chest. Without knowing why, she began to cry silently, and resting her head on her knees, her eyes closed, she let a flood of memories wash over her: the empty lot on Chicago's South Side, little crippled Tonky with his worn-out crutches barely held together with tape. Dear, dear Tonky, where was he now, what had happened to him? What had happened to their little garden and her poor stunted little crab apple, crushed and broken on a pile of rubble in a ten-wheeler? It all seemed so lost and so, so far away, so awfully *gone* and untouchable.

Rachel found her sitting there some minutes later and could see that she had been crying. She sat down besides Kelly on the stone steps and put an arm around her. "Are you okay?"

Kelly heard the real concern and tried to find a response. "Yes, sorry. Silly memories. Sorry."

"Do you want to tell me?"

"Thanks. Not right now." She reached up to take Rachel's hand. "Thank you, Rachel."

"Sure. Whenever, if you want." And then, "Tiggy and I have gossiped ourselves out, so we can leave and go home whenever you feel like it." She gave Kelly's shoulder a quick hug and went back into the little house.

On the drive back over the rolling South Downs they were both silent and at dinner their talk was slightly constrained, Rachel afraid to open a wound, Kelly still slightly embarrassed by Rachel finding her in tears.

But long after they had done the dishes and tidied up and headed for bed, Kelly felt a growing torment. Going upstairs, Rachel had said, "I'm exhausted," and had disappeared into her four poster almost immediately and was soon asleep. But Kelly, equally tired but still dressed, sat on the edge of her bed in the little spare room, unconsciously toying with an expensive gold bracelet. She had taken it off several days ago and left it on her bedside table. It was a constant reminder of how very different her lifestyle in New York had been from Rachel's.

After a moment, she put it back in a drawer of the table and, getting undressed and into her nightie, she thought again of Miss Tiggy's little crab apple tree. It had opened a wound, long buried, but there was far more that was equally upsetting. Rachel's kindness and her sitting on the steps and putting an arm around her shoulders had brought a growing awareness of something Kelly never thought she would accept—Rachel's nonwriting persona, her simple way of life, her clear disdain of wealth and fame. All that, yes, but even more disturbing, far more, was her realization of Rachel's overwhelming greatness as a writer.

Words and thoughts she had read in Rachel's manuscript poured mercilessly through her mind, turning, in comparison and with an almost sickening awareness, her own so-called stellar writing into shallow unimportance. All her best-sellers, her stories, stories, stories created and carefully slanted to sell to women readers, seemed a hollow mockery. If she stopped writing tomorrow, would anyone remember anything she'd ever written? Or care? Would she herself give a damn?

Vague memories stirred of the teacher in community college, his half joking aside that writing was a path to fame and fortune for some, and that she had a better shot at it than most because she wrote so well and so easily. And later his suggesting that she slant whatever she wrote to women. "Your sex is a much bigger market place," he'd said. "There's big money there."

She'd picked up on that, yes, but something else forever nagged, something in her more meaningful than money that had brought her to writing and to having the armor against ever again living the utter misery of what her life had been. But what? Something deep in her, she knew. There, but maddeningly elusive. Trying to think what it was, she'd find herself in an emotional turmoil of dark confusion she couldn't make sense of and which would all suddenly blank out as if whatever was disturbing her didn't want to be discovered.

Getting into bed and before turning off the light, she glanced at her little traveling clock. It was only five minutes to nine, and she couldn't help think that in New York she had almost never gone to bed before eleven, and if she'd dined out somewhere of an evening it had rarely been before midnight. At nine o'clock she had often checked on Gerald, and thinking about him again, she knew he somehow had to be part of her armoring herself with money and success. Not the way he was now, a vegetable, a room away from hers in New York. But Gerald when he and she began. Where had he fitted in? And why? She'd told David Hahn she kept him because he shouldn't lie there unloved. Had she really meant that? She felt a deep pang of unease there, a vague feeling of guilt. But why? He was her husband; she'd married him. And loved him.

Or had she? Remembering their meeting, their dating, their wedding, had she actually loved? Or had there been some other reason for their marriage? Dully she realized now that there had been, that part of her wanting to marry Gerald was knowing that being his wife would put her in a social class above most people and almost untouchable.

Her last thought, as she finally turned off the light and let the darkness and silence of the quiet countryside embrace her, was the irony of that, of seeing Gerald as part of her armor of protection when instead he had been just the opposite. What had happened in Argentina hadn't destroyed her love for him, as people thought, as she had thought herself, because she had never loved him in the first place. She had used Gerald just the way she had used writing her books for women. Gerald was part of the need deep in her to protect something long ago that she couldn't identify.

SEVENTEEN

✦

Gerald used a loose sharp-edged stone to scratch on the side of the cave near the tiny, disguised hole that was the cave's sole entrance the number of days they'd been captive—fourteen. The two weeks had affected the personal states of everyone. In the close quarters and extreme discomfort, the lack of adequate food and sleep due to the bitter mountain cold at night, nerves had become frayed and tempers were on edge. Everyone had lost weight, Castenelli was skeletal, there was no bathing. Body sweat and dirt added to general discomfort while none of the men could shave and had grown beards. Jake had tried crawling out to get an idea of where they were and collect a few sticks to make a fire with. Warning shots that spurted up dirt and rock chips only inches from his head put an end to any further venture.

There was not enough light in the cave to see any

distance from the entrance, and they had blindly rigged one of the half-dozen torn and dirty blankets their captors had thrown in to them across the back of the cave as a shield to hide the only possible toilet, a narrow crevasse in the cave's rocky floor that Jake had found by feeling around slowly on his hands and knees. The ever increasing stench from it permeated everywhere, and they had staked out individual areas for sleep as far from it as possible. There were no mattresses, only the blankets, one for each person, and the floor of the cave was hard shelf.

Daytimes were spent in miserable anxiety and speculation, nights in shivering misery. Teresa openly sought warmth by curling up against Gerald. Castenelli's haughty vows of a terrible revenge on their captors had finally been reduced to his usual sullen and disdainful silence. Sharing mutual disaster had not changed his personality or attitude. For all the dire circumstances, he remained true to form and separate and aloof from the others, even from Teresa, whom he had clearly dismissed now she could in no way be of any use to him.

Gerald had barely finished scratching on the cave's wall and commenting on the date when a sound outside the cave warned him that one of their captors approached. Gerald crawled back into the gloom as the man appeared, swarthy, almost stunted with excessively long and muscular arms, with unkempt hair, a four day stubble and brown teeth from chewing tobacco. He had a handgun tucked in his waistband

and a machete slung over one shoulder. He wordlessly pushed through the cave entrance a webbed sling containing four tin containers, each filled with a greasy soup and a potato, their daily fare. This time, along with the containers, there was a ragged, much read issue of one of Argentina's more luridly sensational newspapers. Hands, Gerald's and Jakes, grasped at it eagerly, both calling Teresa to translate.

She got close to the light at the cave's entrance and quickly scanned the paper. "It's about us," she said.

"What, what?"

"They've got the army looking for us. We're all over every page. And oh, God, How awful. Oh, no, no."

"What?"

"They found poor Gino. They cut his throat."

There was a moment when everyone looked at each other. Gerald said, "Christ, the poor little bugger," and Teresa, freed when captured to feel any obligation toward Castenelli, who showed no sign of emotion, cried at him shrilly. "Don't you care? You rotten son of a bitch. He slaved for you."

There was no reply. Castenelli remained stiffly silent. "Clearly not, you bastard," Teresa said. Sniffing back tears, she returned to the newspaper and scanning several pages said brokenly, "Argoronorte is offering a huge reward to anyone who knows anything." She broke off a moment and then said, "Oh, shit."

"What?"

For the first time in days, she smiled. "They've got me and Gerald having a torrid affair."

"Damn," Gerald said. "Where the hell did they get that?" Ignoring Teresa, he looked accusingly at Jake. "For Christ's sake. I'll be done with Kelly, if it gets to the American papers."

"They didn't get it from me," Jake snapped. "If that's what you were thinking. You weren't exactly discreet about it. Cleaning ladies, night security guards. Maybe Gino seeing a chance for revenge, the way he was always treated." He nodded at a silent Castenelli.

"Oh, look, look," Teresa exclaimed. "Ransom. Now they want another million, and in U.S. dollars, to set us free. That makes six. Four for Castenelli and the rest for the rest of us. "She lowered the paper to stare scornfully at the Italian. "Like you were worth something? What a joke."

The remainder of the day was spent sharing the paper. With only Teresa speaking Spanish, the men could but look at pictures and try to make out the occasional word. They ate their cold, rancid meals in silence, each with his own thoughts until suddenly, toward evening, there were voices and three of the miners appeared. While two stood just outside the cave's entrance, a third, his automatic revolver menacing, crawled in. He pointed to Castenelli. *"Tú!"* he barked roughly. *"Maldito capitalista! Han pagado tu rescate. Andando!"*

When Castenelli didn't move, the miner laughed. He seized the Italian by the hair, yanked him onto his face, and clubbed him across the neck with the butt of the handgun. Then, with Castenelli only half conscious and unresisting, his torn and soiled pajama bottoms down around his ankles, he was hauled and pushed out of the cave.

Teresa cried out, "Gerald, we're ransomed. Come on. We're free," and went to follow, with Jake and Gerald crawling after her. She was blocked when almost all the way through the cave's tiny entrance.

"*Tú, no. Date media vuelta.*" In Spanish the meaning was clear to Jake and Gerald. But Teresa kept screaming, "*Dijo que había pagado el rescate,*" and crawling forward until she received a heavy kick in her face and a volley of unintelligible Spanish. Ignoring it, she struggled to sit, crying now in English. "You said we were ransomed." She tried to rise, her face bloodied.

"Not you. Just him. *Tú, no. Sólo ése.*" The miner said it in English, then Spanish, and laughed and pointed at the naked, crumbled figure of Castenelli.

Jake, ahead of Gerald and nearly out of the cave himself, saw Teresa's desperate grab at the legs of the miner, heard her sobbing cry of "No, no. Us too. *Nosotros también,*" and then saw the vicious cut of the razor sharp machete which half severed her arm. Later he was to remember seeing Castenelli pulled to his feet and being dragged down the hillside, but at that awful instant he could only see Teresa lying in a bubbling pool of her own blood with he and Gerald for the moment helpless to help.

EIGHTEEN

❖

Although Kelly was up and about, Dr. Rice was firm in insisting she not rush back to the States. "You had a near knockout punch, Kelly. We don't want you in some ICU in New York, which is what could happen if you overdo it and relapse. Pneumonia is unforgiving. Unless you have urgent business in New York, stay put a week more."

More importantly, Rachel had agreed with him and urged her not to rush off until certain she felt herself again.

Accompanying Rachel most of each day, either working with her in the garden, helping her to tend the sheep and chickens, or out and around the area lending a hand to friends and neighbors needing help with livestock or with house and farm problems, Kelly wondered when Rachel ever had found the time to write a book. She marveled at the depth of the community life

Rachel led and her down-to-earth ability to do almost anything, from roofing to plumbing repairs and minor doctoring of animals. She still saw no writing at all, however, other than the occasional letter to the London *Times* or a brief essay to the *London Review of Books*. She found that puzzling. She couldn't think of any other successful writer who led the same kind of life. Knowing Rachel was planning another book, she had to conclude that while pencil and paper lay idle on her little writing table, Rachel, like herself, was probably writing endless amounts in her head, sorting out people and plot before putting anything down on paper. Many other writers, Kelly knew, did huge amounts of work when busy doing things that had nothing to do with writing at all.

As she eagerly pored through Rachel's great work, the page after page of foolscap crammed with Rachel's small, neat handwriting with hardly a cross-out or marginal note to be seen, it was almost impossible to believe that ignoring computers, even typewriters, Rachel had laboriously handwritten the entire thousand-odd pages of the masterwork. Caught up in reading about the rise and fall of so many people under so many different circumstances brought on by the dreadful carnage of World War One and an analysis, through the many characters and their fates, of what was perhaps one of the greatest social and economic upheavals in history, Kelly also studied, and as a writer herself, what she saw as Rachel's extraordinary construction in plot development, not just for one protagonist but for many interwoven together, each carefully constructed in depth. There were elements in the way Rachel put things together and held suspense that she'd seen elsewhere in the works of other great writers: Hugo, Tolstoy, George Eliot, Balzac. There was evidence everywhere in the work, also, of Rachel's Cambridge education in the painstaking and endless historical research she must have done.

Excitement grew in Kelly until one morning as she and Rachel breakfasted together she was unable to contain herself. She burst out unexpectedly, "Rachel, I have a confession to make. I've been reading your handwritten manuscript of *The Spoils of War*. I hope that doesn't make you angry with me."

She held her breath while Rachel slowly lowered her coffee cup from her lips, stared at her so intently that for a moment Kelly thought she hadn't heard, and then burst out laughing. "Oh, Kelly, I do love you. You are so guileless sometimes. Did you think I didn't *know* you'd been reading me? And guess what—I've been reading you, too, or more accurately, *read* you. I read two of your novels before you ever came over. And you don't need to tell me, if you're going to, that I'm a damn good writer. I know that myself," she laughed again, "even if everyone says so. What I want to know is, how many people tell you the same?"

She held up a warning hand. "Stop! I don't mean to flatter you about being a best-seller and all that, praise heaped on all the stories you tell for romantically starved middle-aged women of which there seem to be money-paying legions. I mean compliment your actual writing: the way you put things together, Kelly, your airtight plots, your in-depth characterizations, your descriptions." She paused and then said, I know you well enough now, I hope, to candidly say two things. And this, Kelly, is from one writer, always critical, to another. One is that you are a remarkably good writer yourself. Every aspect of every one of your novels shrieks it out. That's one thing. The other thing is this." She fixed Kelly with a hard direct look and said very firmly, "Why on earth do you waste so much ability, so much craftsmanship, and so much great talent writing so much goddamned garbage?"

It took Kelly's breath away. Rachel's coffee cup, headed back to her lips, seemed a sort of a giant exclamation point. Her thoughts tumbled and raced. Did Rachel know, could she *possibly* know, that she had started asking herself the same question? That because of what she'd seen in Rachel's writing that she'd come to face that she was writing garbage purely to make money? And, more importantly because of Rachel and being so unexpectedly thrust into Rachel's way of life, Rachel's thoughts and attitudes, that she had begun to ask herself why? And had come to conclusions that were nothing short of personally shattering.

There was a silence. She found herself averting Rachel's direct gaze, staring at her plate and the still unfinished pancakes Rachel had made for breakfast and feeling an almost overwhelming guilt. Then she looked up. It wasn't the moment to fence or hedge. She had to be honest. She was hardly talking to a fool. "I don't know, Rachel. I … I've started asking myself the same question. Your writing has made me do so. I don't think I hold a candle to your ability, even though you may think so, but I do know that I write garbage. Why? Because it makes me a huge success. That's something I know. But why?"

She pushed back from the table and looked earnestly at Rachel, her expression pained and questioning. "Why do I feel such a compelling need to be a huge success? I cleaned up with my first big publication. And second. Why do I keep needing more and more success on top of them? What is it that drives me? To keep on writing books I don't believe in? I don't know, but I think it has something to do with when I was a child. But that's unreasonable. People grow up, don't they? Get over childish hang-ups? Or maybe I didn't. I just don't know. I simply don't. But I do know that I am suddenly terribly, terribly tired of it all."

Rachel rose, collecting dishes to be washed. "You'll find out, Kelly. You've half the battle won." She laughed as she started washing up and added, "You know, you remind me of myself when I was mid-twenties. Suddenly coming to my senses and struggling to find out why I'd been on such a wrong tack. It was about writing and when I was living with my sister."

Kelly took her the rest of the breakfast things and automatically started drying, realizing with a slight sense of surprise as she did that until she'd been in Rachel's house, doing dishes was something in her life that had always been done by someone else. Putting away a dish, she said, "Your sister? I didn't know you had one, and I looked up all your background before I came over."

"Most people don't. I've never spoken out about her." Rachel saved two cups and poured both herself and Kelly fresh coffee. "Around here, everyone thinks they know me. All the world out there, too, the media especially. They don't. At heart I have always preferred anonymity, I guess. And I keep Rachel to myself. You're one of the very few, Kelly. You and dear old Ashley. And my wonderful Gaelic poet friend, Emil O'Shaunnesy."

She brought the coffees back to the table and sat down again, nursing hers thoughtfully between both hands as she spoke. "About my sister? Well, we weren't actually sisters, I just thought of her that way. Her name was Ruth, and we were the closest friends imaginable. We met in our second year at Cambridge and from day one were inseparable. We couldn't live without each other. When we left university we found homes together, 'digs' as the English say. No, we weren't lovers, although I've nothing against women who are. It was all intellectual. I read English, Ruth read history. The two blended beautifully. Boys? Oh, there were plenty of them. It was the roaring seventies, remember. We burned our bras and got into bed with anyone with whom we cared to indulge ourselves." She laughed. "I even remember sharing one with her and comparing notes—I know, shame on us, but that's the way it was back then."

She paused. Her laughter died. "But it didn't last. Nothing ever does. Oddly, it wasn't because Ruth came from the highest of high. Her father owned a stately home with forty bedrooms and a staff of twenty-five. Her titled mother had lined up a half-dozen young men of her own ilk for her to marry, and she knew she faced disgrace in their eyes and possible disinheritance for taking up with me. Even though I was at Cambridge and a good student, I was Welsh—a dirty word to some English—and no matter how good my own family, they were disdained as out of the loop of academia.

"Surprisingly, we weathered all that with ease, even though they also decided I was evilly leading their daughter into ruin. Our problem was much deeper, and my fault. It was something I didn't recognize until long after it had destroyed our friendship, and Ruth more than me, and ..." Rachel hesitated, and took a deep breath as though having to face something always to be avoided, and Kelly saw deep sadness in her face. "And because after we split up, she went straight down-hill. She drank terribly and surrendered to her parents' snobbery and married some awful society fellow she had nothing in common with. It ... it was too much for her, and a few years later she killed herself."

"Oh, Rachel, I'm sorry ... it must have been terribly painful." Kelly felt a hurt for Rachel she'd never felt for anyone, and wondered if she dared ask Rachel what she had done. While they then silently drank their coffee and with Rachel starting to make a list of what groceries she needed to purchase, she suddenly determined to. "Rachel, Ruth and you. What happened that split you up?"

Rachel hesitated a moment, staring at the list as though reaching a decision. Then she looked up. "What happened?" She laughed suddenly, and her laugh was self-deprecating and had a touch of bitter irony. She said, "I wrote."

Kelly didn't understand. It didn't make sense. "You what?"

"I wrote. Oh, I don't mean the putting it down on paper part. I mean all the rest of the twenty-four hours when I wrote in my head. It meant that when we were together I wasn't with her at all, I cut her out completely. She felt it, the sheer loneliness of it. When we were together she was actually alone. She actually wasn't with me because I wasn't there—I was some-place else. I was in the damn novel I was writing. It … it drove her half crazy. It had turned me into someone who didn't share, didn't communicate anymore. I had become in her eyes someone who didn't care. Not for anybody or anything except myself. And especially not for her. It destroyed what had been *us,* and that killed her."

Even before she finished speaking, Kelly felt the darkness of guilt creep up through her again. Wasn't this what Jake had told her? Or tried to? Jake had said that Gerald was lonely and, looking back in the long silence after Rachel finished speaking, she real-ized she had done the same thing to Gerald. Gerald hadn't killed himself; he was too filled with life for that.

Instead, he had found solace with other women. She'd driven Gerald to infidelity. The guilt wasn't with him, it was with her.

A question in her stirred, and she felt the confidence to ask it. "Rachel, is that why you never married?"

"No, not at all. I almost did marry later. I fell quite in love. Desperately, actually. His name was Robert. Everyone called him Robbie, and he was a wonderful guy. But at the last moment he preferred someone else."

Kelly said, "Oh, gosh, Rachel, I'm sorry."

Rachel said wanly, "I guess you can't win everything, right? But perhaps it was just as well. I might have done the same thing to him that I did to Ruth."

Kelly toyed with her coffee cup a moment, staring into it, and then looked up at Rachel, seeing Rachel's aging in her wispy gray hair and the lines beginning to etch her face, and realizing how painful age must make some memories. She said, "I'm glad we talked. You and Ruth. How you killed your friendship. It explained so much to me about my marriage."

"Tell me."

Kelly did. In the intimacy of talking to Rachel and with Rachel revealing so much of her own personal self, she felt a sense of relief that was almost exhilarating. Unrestrained, she poured out to Rachel first all that lay behind the lurid headlines of Argentina; about living with Gerald with twenty-four-hours-a-day nurses. "I think I know now why I keep him," she said. "Guilt. I drove him to Teresa or whatever her name was. Poor woman. Jake said she was nice, actually. I've stop hating her. She wasn't to blame for his cheating. I was. All my anger was because Gerald's infidelity had threatened the pristine, safe world I had made for myself."

She went on, her sense of relief growing, and told Rachel then about her childhood, about never having known her parents. "I have no idea who they were," she said, laughing briefly. "It was foster homes almost from day one and a different school with each. And there wasn't any aunt. There was a little boy at one school who was picked up and walked home every day by someone he called Aunt something-or-other. She always smiled at me and said "Hello," and one day when it was very hot she bought me an ice cream cone. I'd never had one before. She was so nice. So for years I made up an aunt who raised me and who I used to imagine was just like her.

"Until the welfare people let me go, and I was free of all the social workers and able to change my name and create an entirely new life for myself, my only escape, my only safety, was in an empty city lot where I wasn't allowed."

The persistent darkness of her memories of Chicago, of Tonky and their garden and the crab apple, that at Tiggy's had almost overwhelmed her, now magically started to lift away. For the first time ever, she spoke freely about how in the lot she was able, through the love she felt there, to escape from all the hatred and anger, even for a short time. "I dreamed back then that someday I would have a new life of my own," she said, "when every day I'd be safe to feel the way I felt back then. But I knew, even though I was just a child, that I would have to be rich to do it, rich and successful like the people I saw in the better suburbs of Chicago, like Lincoln Park where I said I was raised—a lie, of course—or really rich, like people in Lake Forest and Winnetka. But when I actually *was* rich, all that love that was in me in that lot, the *real* me, a child who cared about things that were important, ironically became lost, buried under the very money and success I'd sought to keep it safe."

She was silent a moment and then said, "I didn't know that until now—until I came here. It's why I was crying in Miss Tiggy's garden. Seeing her little tree brought it all back, and so unexpectedly." She took a deep breath and looked at Rachel with a wry smile. "And then, talking to you, I suddenly began to realize the truth about myself, and I don't know whether to laugh at myself now or cry some more for all the lost years."

"Sad," Rachel said. "You thought that the end would justify the means. It never does. Not ever. But Kelly, you will rediscover everything within you that empty lot meant, and probably when you least expect it. I promise you will." Then she said, "I guess there's a hell in life for everyone. You look at a complete stranger—a seemingly happy one—and you have to wonder. What did they have to suffer?" She laughed. "It's the great leveler. We all share something in common. It makes us all terribly equal."

She rose and put her shopping list in her pocket.

"And don't worry. You've won half the battle realizing that you've been doing what you shouldn't be. In your writing, I mean. You'll have a spell, maybe a year or two, feeling cut adrift, and then you'll settle into writing whatever isn't garbage, even if perhaps not so lucrative. Don't push it. It will come to you. Guaranteed. You're a writer, Kelly, a bloody good one, and writers don't simply dry up and blow away. Not the real ones like you."

She let the thought hang and then said, "And now come give me a hand getting the sheep out to pasture. I can hear them already getting shamefully restless, silly fools that they are."

Kelly smiled, feeling a rush of sudden warmth, took a last swallow of coffee and followed her out of the house.

NINETEEN

✦

Together, Jake and Gerald managed to drag Teresa back inside the cave and found her left arm half severed above the elbow. She had machete cuts, too, on both hands from holding them out in defense. The blow to her arm hadn't reached the main artery, and after they had stripped off her clothes to use as bandages and bound the arm protectively close to her body, and had stopped the flow of blood from it and from a huge machete gash across her throat that had just missed the jugular, they wrapped her in two blankets, her own and Castenelli's. She was only half conscious and in shock and so not feeling too much pain. That would come later, Jake knew.

As evening fell and with Teresa moaning feverishly, he and Gerald tried to assess their situation. Teresa couldn't possibly last more than a few days, but there was no way they could get her down off the rocky hills to medical help.

"That bastard Castenelli," Gerald said at one point during the night. "If we ever get out of here, I'm going to have a field day with the media. Sitting here for two weeks knowing he was going to walk free and leaving us stuck. And with a woman, too. With all his millions the son of a bitch couldn't pay our ransom along with his? Or at least hers after he brought her here. It defies thought." He was silent a moment and then said, "Jesus Christ, where the hell are we anyway? The newspaper said the Army was out looking for us, why the hell haven't they found us?"

Jake said, "They will eventually." And wondered if they ever would.

"Yeah, sure. Eventually. And in time to find three rotting corpses."

Jake didn't reply. Teresa's condition had made him feel doubly desperate. They simply had to get out of there. Somehow. They couldn't just do nothing and die. He had a thought and wondered why he hadn't had it before. He asked suddenly, "Why would they have more than one guy guarding this place?"

"What are you saying?"

"When they dragged off Castenelli there were two of them, but I think there's only one guarding us all the time. The same guy every day, the one who brings us our food. I recognized his boots. They don't match. I think someone, maybe several or one of them, brings our food up to him and then shoves off again."

"They were silent a while and then Gerald added,

"Maybe you're right about that. Just one guarding us. When that guy comes tomorrow with our food I'm going to take a chance."

"Like what?"

"Grab his legs of the one who stays here and upend him and try to get his gun. He has one, I saw it. An AK-47 semi. When he clobbered Teresa with his machete he had it leaning up against a rock a couple of feet away."

Jake said, "I think we ought to draw lots on that." He groped around and found some dry grass and closed a fist around two pieces of it with just the two ends sticking up. "Short one goes at him first, okay?"

"Sounds right." Gerald pulled a piece of grass lose from Jake's fist. Jake revealed the other. He had the long gone, Gerald the short.

"Worth the try," Gerald said.

They didn't talk further but tried to make Teresa as comfortable as they could, giving her the last of their canteen water. Morning found them red-eyed from lack of sleep and their nerves taut from waiting for their captor to appear. It was almost noon when he did and Gerald, face close to the tiny entrance said, "You were right. There's two. One's brought it up and he's given it to the other, and he's headed off."

"Good luck," Jake said. I'll be right behind you."

He'd hardly spoken when Gerald muttered "Here goes …" and threw himself through the narrow cave entrance, reaching out to grasp their startled captor's legs, jerking him upward and off balance. And then everything happened so fast that Jake could hardly remember how it played out: their captor scrambling up, clubbing Gerald on the head with his semiautomatic rifle butt as Gerald struggled to rise, himself hung up on the branch hiding the cave's entrance, then finally free and outside and going for the miner who was clubbing Gerald again and again, himself trying to wrench the AK-47 away and the miner, swinging the semi's butt around, slamming it into his face before he could rise, then slashing at him with his machete. In the pain and surprise of the machete there was a moment of sheer terror before, half blinded, he grappled desperately, bringing the miner face down into the rocky rubble. He got an arm locked around the man's neck and across his throat and his knee into the man's back until he felt the man's neck snap and his body go limp.

It seemed forever until he could find the strength to rise. He kept thinking, "If any of the others come, I'm done for." He felt sick with fear. But there was no one. A birdcall eerily broke the total silence of the hillside. He felt his face. Blood poured, and his fingers following the machete across his cheek and nose felt his eye and found it crushed. For moments the pain was everything until through a growing numbness he realized where he was and that he couldn't stay there. He had to leave, find help somewhere. He looked around and through a red haze of blood saw Gerald only a few feet away. He lay inert, his motionless head in a small pool of blood. Jake thought, "When they come back they'll kill him." He couldn't leave him. And Teresa? He couldn't leave her either. But he couldn't take both with him, and she was probably too badly hurt to move. She'd only survive if he could get help soon enough. She had to. "Don't die, Teresa," he thought. "Don't die. I'll get help."

He ripped off the miner's belt and tied Gerald's wrists together, and then crawled beneath him and got his head up through the loop Gerald's arms made and started off, half crouched, sometimes on his hands and knees and sometimes standing, dragging Gerald on his back and using the AK-47 to pull and balance himself.

The boulder-strewn hillside was steep. He headed down, crawling, sliding, falling, tearing himself against sharp rocks and rubble, his shorts ripped away. And suddenly when he felt he couldn't go on, that he'd have to leave Gerald, he felt water in his face. He'd come onto a small stream.

He was lying, face half in it, his blood turning the water rushing around it crimson, and pinned down by Gerald when the small patrol of soldiers found him.

TWENTY

Kelly found herself dreading having to leave Brill-on-Marsh and Rachel. Every day was escape from facing new doubts and, in spite of Rachel's optimism, anxieties about her life and where she was going. She knew she had drawn a line she would never cross—writing any more books for millions of admiring women readers. Yet she remained indecisive about what she *would* write. And indecisive, too, about her non-writing life. What about Gerald and her apartment in New York, and then New York itself, with its crowds and ugliness and xenophobia? It all seemed completely alien now, even offensive—Phil Townsend, Arson McKain, the apartment, her daily routine. Only Estella and Mischief remained in her heart. The time came, however, when she knew she couldn't put off going back any longer, and she called Clarissa Chatterly and asked her to book a flight in a few days' time.

When she told Rachel, Rachel was silent a long moment. They were both puttering in the vegetable patch, weeding out amidst some burgeoning radishes and chatting about locals and what they would eat for dinner. Rachel put down her trowel and sat back and, after wiping the back of one grimy gloved hand across her forehead, she said, "Oh, dear." And then was silent for a moment before she resumed work and said, "Yes, I suppose you have to, but I'm going to miss you."

"I'll come back."

"Do."

Nothing more was said, but as she continued her weeding Rachel felt more and more the warmly comfortable closeness of Kelly's presence. She thought suddenly again of Ruth. Kelly wasn't Ruth; she was a different person. She was Kelly, but she realized with an odd sense of surprise, as though discovering something always there but never noticed, that she had all the same feelings for Kelly that she'd had so many years ago for Ruth—love, respect, safety, all the goodness of having a trusted "sister." As the past rushed back into her memory, she glanced over at Kelly who, oblivious to her thoughts, was earnestly struggling with a reluctant-to-leave clump of wild daisies that had somehow found their way in amongst the radishes. Her presence, Rachel knew, had changed everything. It had made her realize how all the long years since Ruth had gone and she'd also lost Robert had been empty ones. She had worked, she had produced and been successful, she had settled into a community she cared deeply about.

But something had been missing that she had forced herself to ignore—the warmth and love she had all-so-briefly shared. Now, completely unforeseen, it had come back with Kelly, and Rachel saw how lonely she must have been, a loneliness that she had stoically accepted as simply the way life was.

Watching Kelly struggle with the unwanted weed, she suddenly didn't want her to go. She didn't want to have to face that lonely emptiness again. She remembered that Tiggy had told her she was planning to sell her little cottage and move to Cornwall to live with her bachelor brother. "I'm getting too old for this, Rachel," she'd said, hanging a fresh-washed sheet up to dry in the sun.

"I'll buy Tiggy's house myself," Rachel thought. "And it will be there for Kelly. She might not want to spend all her time here, but it would be a start even if she only uses it as a vacation home." She'd tell Kelly tonight, she decided, and feeling a whole different person and flushed with a kind of happiness that had become almost alien to her, she went back to work weeding.

At lunch she said, "I hate weepiness. I think we ought to have a celebration. Be positive. Be *us*. Uppercase. Writers united or something like that. Champagne. To hell with more weeding this afternoon, and I'm out of the heavenly stuff, so let's go into Chichester and get some. Good idea?"

Kelly laughed. "I second it." She'd hesitated to tell Rachel, but now the genie was out of the bottle, she felt a heavy load off her heart. Rachel's understated British reaction to her news that she was booked to fly back to the States told her more than anything of the fondness that had grown between them. Rachel, she knew, was going to miss her as much as she was going to miss Rachel. When it came to the actual moment of parting, she determined she'd would do everything not to cry and to match what she knew would be Rachel's typical constraint, no matter her feelings.

"And you could do your gift shopping while we're there," Rachel said. "For Estella and Mischief. Save scurrying about in London or paying high prices for jams in Fortnum or Harrods when there's an excellent jam shop in Chichester I know of."

They finished off a bottle of white wine and did the dishes, and then after tidying up they set off in Rachel's clunky old Land Rover, chased for a while by Ophelia until Rachel stopped and, getting out, sternly ordered her to go home.

In town, Kelly found exactly what would be perfect for Estella, and trying not to have her purchases be too forcible a reminder of the unwanted everything she was returning to, she also picked up a few touristy things celebrating the South Downs for several of the more regular nurses.

At the wine shop, suitably announced over its door in bold raised letters as The Beloved Grape, Rachel said, "Shall we do French? Or would you prefer Californian? I'd suggest British but unfortunately we haven't got the hang of being truly civilized yet."

"Why not both?"

"Get hopelessly tiddly? Kelly, you are pure genius."

Laughing, they exited the shop and, arms linked, headed for the Land Rover parked across the busy street and only yards away, Rachel happily clutching the two bottles of champagne and Kelly lugging a shopping bag full of presents. They waited on the curb a moment while a huge truck rumbled by and then Rachel stepped firmly forward and around the back of it and right into the path of a car in the oncoming lane. The sickening sound of impact, the too-late shriek of hard-braked tires, and for a moment an awful silence until somewhere someone screamed. Kelly dropped her carry bag and rushed to Rachel, who lay crumpled and inert amidst the shattered glass of the champagne bottles.

"Rachel. Oh, my God, Rachel." She fell to the ground by Rachel and held Rachel's head in her lap. And helplessly began to wipe away the blood bubbling from Rachel's mouth. "No, no. Rachel! Help someone, please. Help!"

Others knelt beside Kelly, strangers pressed around, shocked silent at what they'd seen. Someone spread a coat over Rachel. The driver who had hit her, a young woman, stood crying helplessly. There were sirens. An ambulance came, then police, moving people back. Medics took over. Rachel was put on a stretcher and the stretcher slid into the ambulance. Someone helped Kelly in. The doors closed and the ambulance moved away.

In it, a medic patched into the hospital with a report as he simultaneously placed an oxygen cone over Rachel's face, ran an emergency IV line, and then listened to Rachel's heart with a stethoscope. After a moment, he put the stethoscope away and turned off the oxygen and leaned back. "You a relative, Miss?"

"Friend." She looked at him and then down at Rachel and knew Rachel was gone.

⯈ ⯇

Word had got out that the woman struck down on a street in Chichester was the world-renowned British author, Rachel Sommerset. The media, never slow with a celebrity tragedy, were at the hospital almost as soon as the ambulance arrived there. Kelly, in a state of shock and only beginning to fully understand what had happened, found herself in the emergency room with Rachel, with Rachel's inert body on a stretcher and with nurses and doctors removing IV lines and vital signs monitors no longer of any use.

Standing, looking at Rachel, she had but one thought and one emotion. This was Rachel lying there. But *not* Rachel. Someone else. Rachel was gone. But that couldn't be. That was impossible. And yet it was. Rachel wasn't like Gerald, in a coma but still alive. Rachel was dead. Numbly she just stood and stared until a sheet was pulled all the way over Rachel and she was wheeled away. Nurses, then a doctor finally took notice of her and gently urged her to leave. One of the police officers who had accompanied her and Rachel into the emergency room took charge. He was a local who lived close to Brill-on-Marsh. He had met Rachel personally several times at The Lamb and knew she had an American writer guest.

"If you come with me, Miss, I'll take you out a side door, less of a mob there, and ride you back home. You won't want to go out front. TV cameras and all. I'm sure you don't feel like that right now."

Too numb to reply, Kelly let him lead her to a police car. He drove her back to Brill-on-Marsh and Rachel's house, but there it was too late to avoid the demanding media a second time. World famous people didn't die in Chichester every day, and certainly not a woman considered a national treasure. A swarm of reporters along with several TV trucks and TV cameramen crowded the road that ran by the house and the front walk, trampling down vegetables and flowers and pressed in around the front door as well. The officer, his arm protectively around Kelly, elbowed and shouldered his way to it, pushing aside cameras and mikes thrust in Kelly's face as they went. The shouted questions from two dozen voices were a confused jumble that Kelly hardly heard—*Were you at the accident? Did she have any last words? Do you know what she was writing? What was she doing in Chichester? Why the champagne, was she planning a party? Did she know she would probably get the Nobel? Are you a personal friend or a relative? Are you that American writer who came over to meet her?*

Until just at the door someone insistently close cried, "What's your name, lady?

She turned then to face the sea of microphones, cameras, and notebooks. There was no way she would ever allow her name, her writing fame in America and the lurid sensationalism of Argentina, to shadow the memory of a great writer like Rachel Sommerset.

"My name is Kaja Arzejwski," she said. And went into the house, closing the door behind her.

TWENTY-ONE

*I*n the next few days, news of Rachel was everywhere. It seemed there was nothing else on television, on the radio, or in the newspapers. Prayers were held for her at several of England's leading churches. There were statements on her life and importance by the palace, the prime minister, and others and personal interviews with great names who had once known or had the luck to meet her. There were interviews with unknown strangers on the street. "Did you read her great work?" There was talk of her Nobel Prize.

At Brill-on-Marsh, friends and neighbors, and many others, came singly and in groups to heap flowers from the door of her house all the way to the road, hundreds and hundreds of bunches of them. There were rows of candles, too, which at night, while some kept vigil, twinkled in the stirring night air like scores of fallen stars. As if to emphasize Rachel's absence, her old Land Rover, brought home by some kindly police officer, stood as usual but now forlornly silent on a little side path of dirt that wrapped around to the back of the house.

The press was still there in force but were kept marshalled at a relatively respectful distance, television trucks and all. Their persistence was a constant annoyance. They badgered every villager or local farmer they could persuade to talk, and in the house the telephone rang off the hook night and day. They had decided Kelly had to be a valuable source of information on Rachel's entire life from the day of her birth, and Kelly felt obliged always to answer the phone in case it wasn't the press but a message from a local, or some other call of importance.

Two days after Rachel died, Kelly was in the kitchen making herself first-of-the-day coffee and some breakfast toast when the phone rang. She muttered, "Oh, damn," and almost didn't answer. Who could it be this time? The press already? She hoped not Arson or Clarissa Chatterly, who mercifully had not yet telephoned. She didn't think she could stand talking to either of them today. She picked up the receiver. "Hello?"

"Miss Anders?" A cultivated English voice she didn't know. Clipped. Educated. An older voice. It didn't sound at all like the press.

"Yes?"

"I haven't had the pleasure of meeting you. I'm Ashley Sims-Hanover. I hope I haven't woken you."

"No, it's all right."

"Sickening, what's happened. Especially terrible for you, I'm sure. I'm so very sorry."

"Thank you. I'm alright." She was still slightly wondering, and then the name suddenly meant something to her. Sir Ashley Sims-Hanover was Rachel's publisher, the head of the giant publishing company the Hanover Group, and one of Rachel's dearest friends. He was also one of the most famous figures in England.

"Look, I hesitated to ask you," he said, "especially at this time, but would it be alright if I came down this morning, late-ish, perhaps around noon? There are several things of Rachel's that are important to us."

"Of course. Can I get you lunch?"

"Oh, dear child, I wouldn't dream of so putting you out. I can just pop into The Lamb on the way should I feel starved. I know it well."

He came early in the afternoon. Kelly had spent the time until he arrived packing and rearranging her bags that Clarissa Chatterley had sent down from London and deciding what she would wear back to New York. "I damn well ought to just go as I am," she thought. Dressing after Sims-Hanover called, she'd put on what had become her daily wear—jeans and a sweat shirt—and had slipped into farm boots. "Except since I'm traveling first class, I'd look a little odd." And that made her think how odd it was to be going back at all, and how strangely distant it all seemed, New York, her apartment. Living with Rachel had killed any liking she might ever have had for any of it. Only

Rachel's home felt safe and familiar.

She'd had a sandwich lunch when she heard the car as it pulled up and, peering through the window, saw a rather run-down looking black Mini stopped in the road. Out of it got an elderly, slightly stooped white-haired man. Casually dressed in unpressed flannels with a worn knee-length suede jacket, he placed a large bouquet of flowers on the mountain of them already there then came to the front door, and when Kelly ran down to open it, she found herself looking at a time-worn graying face beneath an unruly shock of hair that made her think of the benevolent face of a priest she'd once met in Italy when she and Gerald had been newly married.

It was Sir Ashley Sims-Hanover. Pleasantries and deep felt condolences exchanged, and when he was asked his preference, he decided on coffee rather than tea. They sat at the kitchen table and he said, laughing, "I'm like Rachel. I've always thought tea the curse of England. We don't need doctors or medicine here. Just a cup of tea, thank you."

When she'd poured water into the French coffee press and served it to him, he said, "You must wonder why I have come down. What I am after. It's Rachel's original manuscript for *The Spoils of War*. She always said to me that she wanted me to have it if anything happened to her. As I'm sure she told you, we were close friends as well as my being her publisher. With you going back to America, who knows what might happen to it or anything else of hers. Rachel has no living relatives I know of, except some second cousin somewhere, teaching in the North someplace I think. But someone is bound to show up, if nobody other than her solicitors. Besides very great sentimental meaning to me, and although I would never think of selling it, the manuscript has considerable monetary value."

Kelly went and brought down the stack of foolscap and laid it carefully on the kitchen table. "I understand she was writing a new novel," she said.

"That's right. Hasn't a title yet. I think she was toying with *Bryan's Way*, a Joyce stream-of-consciousness sort of thing about a homeless genius roving the countryside and living on handouts—social observation again. Our changing times. It would be in her scrawl again on a thousand million pages like this stack." He smiled wryly. "No computers or even typewriters for our Rachel, bless her. 'They clutter thinking,' she told me. She said she'd done a few chapters and made piles of notes for the rest, but since she is no longer with us, I'm afraid they'd be useless even if we had them."

They talked a while. Rachel, he told her, had much admired her as a writer and become very fond of her, too. A surprise to him because she had dreaded the meeting Arson McKain had talked him and her into. "Scared her witless," he said. "She really didn't want to meet you automatically at all. She took to people—you saw that—but rarely closely, but then there was your unfortunate illness which gave her the chance to know you personally. She said you had the right chemistry for her—her words exactly. She hadn't felt such an affinity for another woman since the friend who was a sister to her passed on. Well, I'm sure she told you all about that."

"Yes, she did," Kelly said.

"Places you among the very privileged few. I'm sorry not to have seen more of you."

In a letter to her solicitor, Rachel had requested cremation and that her ashes be privately scattered somewhere on the South Downs, and before he left, Sims-Hanover said, "I won't be coming down for her ashes tomorrow. I'm most unfortunately due in Berlin and can't break it. So I won't see you again. But keep in touch, do. If you should ever want to send a manuscript to us, address it to me personally. I'll be more than glad to read anything you write."

Kelly promised she would and thought his offer especially courteous since she knew he would consider any of the genre she wrote in beneath his publishing company.

The following day and in the absence of any relatives, her solicitors, with police help, managed to persuade the press to keep their distance, and Kelly, along with a score of local friends, gathered on a wide expanse of the verdant South Downs, grazed on by scattered flocks of sheep. Tommy, the publican, spoke briefly with tears in his eyes about her life among them and the debt they all owed her very existence. Then all stood silent while a black-robed bearded priest from the local church, a large wooden crucifix hanging from his corded belt, said prayers she had requested.

Michael Potter and another farmer friend took turns scattering her ashes, and after a few minutes' reverent silence, everyone drifted away. It was all over.

TWENTY-TWO

Over … and yet Kelly felt it wasn't. Something was amiss. It gave her a restless night, but first thing in the morning, she made up her mind to set things right. After she'd had coffee and some toast, she got dressed in her now habitual work clothes and went out and got into the Land Rover. The keys were on the driver's seat, and the old vehicle reluctantly clunked to life, as it always did, and as though nothing had happened.

It was only eight thirty, but at The Lamb both Tommy and his rotund little wife were in their shirt-sleeves, cleaning up after last night and readying for their long day's work. They looked up, surprised, as Kelly pulled up a bar stool and sat.

"Good morning, Miss."

"Good morning. Tommy. I know you're not open, but could I have a shot of something?"

"Coming up. And I should think you probably need

one." He poured her out some of his best brandy and put it down in front of her. "There you go." He watched while Kelly had a first few sips and then said, "It's Miss Anders, is it?"

"Yes."

"The press had you with a different name."

"That was another life."

Tommy knew when not to comment further. He said, "Rachel spoke highly of you. You've had a rough time, Miss. I understand you were with her when it happened."

"Yes." And then, "Tommy, would you care to host a celebration?"

"Miss?"

"At Rachel's house. A get-together, everyone around here. All her friends and neighbors. To celebrate her life, when it meant so much to everyone. I think she would have appreciated it."

The burly publican stared at Kelly an instant and then turned to his wife, who had gone back to setting tables. "Here, luv. Belay all that and lock the door. We've got a big day ahead of us."

Early afternoon, they came in droves, scores of people from miles around the little village of Brill-on-Marsh, working farmers, landed gentry, shopkeepers from Chichester, the local police. The house was packed with them and champagne flowed like water, a dozen cases of it. Plates of food—cold cuts and salads and hot dishes Tommy and his wife had miraculously got together in a few short hours—lined a buffet table and disappeared as fast as they were put down. It was a party Rachel would have loved, Kelly thought. Old friends renewing acquaintances, others swapping gossip. Somewhere in the middle of it, Michael Potter shouted for silence and raised his glass of champagne. "There will only be one toast at this celebration of a great life. To our Rachel, our dearest friend and neighbor. Rachel, we are going to miss you."

There were calls of "hear, hear" and the clinking of scores of glasses between friends, between strangers, until hours later the last person disappeared into the gathering evening.

Tommy and his wife insisted on helping Kelly clean up. "Rachel always kept a tidy house, and we're not going to have you go to bed amidst all this mess." Once satisfied, they stayed a while chatting with Kelly about Rachel and telling some pub stories.

"Will you be going off soon?"

"In a day or so."

"Come back and see us, then."

Kelly promised she would, and when they too left, Kelly was alone. She had wanted all during the celebration to break down and let herself cry, not so much over the terrible loss she felt, the grief that had begun almost to numb her heart, but because of the love she had felt all around her. Her tears would have been partially tears of joy. Sitting in the silent kitchen, she let them flow, and then with a last look around, went upstairs to get herself ready for bed. Her flight back to the States was booked for the day after tomorrow. Arson McKain had long ago gone back to New York and Clarissa Chatterly would come down to Brill-on-Marsh to drive her up to London's Heathrow Airport and to the same old life— her apartment, Gerald, the box of fan letters forwarded every week from McKain's office.

The same, but not the same. Nothing was the same anymore and never would be. As she sat on the edge of the guest room bed in her nightgown, she thought that there was one thing that would stay the same, however, and would always be. It was the part of her that in a short two weeks had become so closely like Rachel. Or indeed perhaps had always been. It was the part of her that her armor of success had sought to protect, and although buried and silently unseen by that success, had somehow remained deep inside her until all that had happened to her at Brill-on-Marsh.

In the morning, she saw Ophelia off in the arms of Michael Potter. "We know each other from way back. Won't be any problem for her to adjust," he said. He would come later for the sheep and chickens and drove off with Ophelia sitting on his lap. Then, feeling completely at odds and ends, Kelly made herself another coffee and started up the stairs with it, intending to get out her laptop and look at her long neglected emails. Half way up, she stumbled, spilling some of the coffee.

With an "Oh, damn," she put the cup down, retrieved a sponge and dishcloth from the kitchen, and began wiping away coffee that had splashed against some of the books lining the staircase wall. Halfway through doing it she suddenly realized that she was dabbing coffee away from a familiar leather cover—one exactly like Rachel's notebook on her worktable by the chimney upstairs. "No," she thought, "it can't be." But it was. When she pulled it out and opened it she saw scrawled in its pages the first six chapters of the book Rachel planned, *Bryan's Way,* and then pages and pages of notes on how Rachel wanted it to develop. Spilled coffee and wiping it up forgotten, Kelly took what was left in her cup upstairs along with the notebook and, sitting at Rachel's writing table, began to read.

Evening was falling, the room darkening, when she closed the notebook and sat back in thought. Everything in her life that had seemed so confused and uncertain, first since Miss Tiggy's, then since Rachel's death, had suddenly become clear. She knew exactly what she had to do, what lay ahead. She would finish Rachel's book for her. It would be a long hard job, but it would be Rachel's words, Rachel's style, and above all, Rachel's book. She could do it, there was no question in her mind that she could. And do it perhaps better than anybody—she felt certain of that. When she finished the job, she'd pack it up and send it off to Sir Ashley with Rachel as the author. She would ask for herself only that she be mentioned in author's acknowledgments as Kaja Arzejwski, a helpful friend.

TWENTY-THREE

Kelly wrapped the notebook carefully in brown paper and for the trip back to New York stowed it for safety at the bottom of her carry-on. She didn't dare take the chance of putting it in her checked baggage—she had once experienced the misery of having baggage lost—and she still felt so nervous about it that twice during the flight across the Atlantic she'd twice felt in the carry-on to make sure it hadn't taken leave somehow by itself or that some fellow passenger had not mysteriously stolen it without her being aware.

Arriving without incident, she placed it on the desk in her New York apartment office. There, and as she stood a moment silently staring at it, she felt as though it was rebuking her, that it was saying, "What am I doing here?" And when she finally tore her eyes from it, all she could think was that something was terribly wrong. Rachel's notebook seemed unreal in the

197

surroundings of her New York apartment. It was part of a completely different life.

Assailed suddenly by a wave of uncertainty, she left it unwrapped on her desk and went from her little office to the living room. She started to make herself a drink, and then thought better of it. A drink was another time. It hadn't fit at Brill-on-Marsh, and now it didn't fit here either, not with the darkness that had suddenly come over her the moment she'd landed and left the plane from England, nor, certainly, when she'd taxied into the city from JFK to be greeted at her building by the usual obsequious doorman and had taken the silent elevator up to the penthouse. Only Estella and Mischief had been welcoming. The confidence she'd felt when discovering Rachel's notebook, all her determination to finish Rachel's novel for her, her certainty that she could do it, had ebbed away. She felt utterly lost.

It was late in the evening, Estella long in bed and, Kelly, sleepless, went to the kitchen and made a coffee. Bringing it back, she sat on the couch with it. Just as she'd feared when in England, the pleasant familiarity of the room was now completely unfamiliar. It was as though she had just walked into it for the first time. The night sky of New York beyond the glass terrace doors was a dull and alien sulfurous mauve. Below it were the myriad, make-believe stars that were the lights of those buildings she could see beyond the strange specter-like ghostly potted trees and plants on her terrace.

It was a different world. Her bedroom was equally

alien. Her big comfortable bed, her French dressing table, the impressionist prints on the walls, her modern, marble-tiled bathroom, all appeared as though not hers but belonging to someone else.

She had hardly been back in New York but a few hours and numbly she realized that even in spite of the loving presence of Estella and Mischief, she herself felt as not belonging there as much as Rachel's still unwrapped notebook. Like the notebook, she was a stranger in her own home.

Her feeling that way was, if anything, made even worse when within days she met with Arson McKain in his spacious office at Crossroads Publishing, with its view of other towering skyscrapers and the crawling streets of Manhattan far below that seemed like distant black snakes. Listening to his perfunctory remarks, "What a perfectly awful time you've had," "Are you fully recovered from it all?" and "How glad you must be to be back home," she heard the emptiness of the words that were thrown out, she knew, for appearances' sake. Arson McKain was as devoid of any true personal feelings for her as she had for him. To him, she was nothing more or less than a commodity.

"What do you have planned for us next, Kelly? In spite of what you have been through, I'm sure you have been conjuring up yet another success."

Looking up at the covers of several of her best-sellers

that were framed and hung on the walls, Kelly had no answer. What would be the point in telling him that she had no intention of ever writing another book for her army of women readers, or for his publishing house?

She covered with platitudes and a smile she didn't feel, and when she was gone, Arson McKain worried. What Kelly had experienced in England had left its mark, he thought. Kelly didn't seem herself at all. She wasn't the confident driving woman he'd come to see her as, one who almost exemplified the sophisticated, polished New York success. She seemed someone else.

On her part, Kelly, returning to her apartment, her taxi snail-pacing its way through the usual sludge and cacophony of New York traffic, was thinking and feeling the same thing. With a jolt while talking to the publisher she realized why, since her return, everything seemed so alien. It was because she was no longer in any way a part of it. She no longer thought or saw things or did things the same way as she once had. It was as if she had become someone else. The few friends she'd talked to, Arson's assistant and the rest of his staff who had gathered in a "welcoming committee"—familiar friendly faces once a pleasure for her to see—were all now people with whom she had no connection. New York had become as foreign as the life she had once lived there.

Her voice mail had been filled with messages from Phil Townsend. The mere thought of him repulsed her, and she dreaded that she might see him again. She'd left emails unanswered, changed her phone number, the lock on her apartment door. She'd given instructions to the doorman downstairs.

And then there was Gerald. She'd seen him the first day she was back. She hadn't wanted to; she'd found the thought of seeing him oddly frightening, as though he might suddenly come awake and, bolting upright, point an accusing finger at her. There was really no way she could not, however. So she'd gone into the sterile little room, and while the nurse, a new one she didn't know, remained silently respectful to one side, she stood by his bed looking down at him. To her surprise she found herself utterly devoid of any feeling. Her thoughts were simply that this wasn't anyone she knew, or had ever known. This was a complete stranger, as alien to her as everyone and anything else.

Now, sitting alone in the living room with her coffee, Mischief curled asleep on the couch next to her, she remembered her interview with David Hahn and saw herself back then as someone it was hard to remember. The Kelly Anders he had interviewed had become to her a near fictitious character. The Kelly Anders today had become Kaja and the little girl who had had found life and hope with Tonky in the cluttered vacant lot in Chicago's South Side.

TWENTY-FOUR

———◆———

She spent a sleepless night, and when day finally came, grudgingly dragged herself to her bank and then to her lawyer on long neglected routine affairs, and then bought a few presents to send back to friends at Brill-on-Marsh: Michael Potter, Tommy and his wife, and above all, Tiggy.

It was an unusually warm day for the late time of year when leaves were turning and frost was settling in the early mornings on the lawns of the city parks. She started to hail a taxi to take her back downtown when on sudden impulse she changed her mind and headed instead for MOMA, the Museum of Modern Art, only a short walk away. She'd seen an ad in the *New York Times* for a photo exhibit there. It was for an exhibit of the assembled work of the photographer Jake Barlow that rewarded him for his years of nomadic wandering. It featured, amidst some war-torn ruins, a woman clutching her two small children as they faced an ISIS firing squad. Around them were the splayed and crumpled bodies of other women and children already gunned down.

Jake and everything he represented seemed to Kelly so very long ago, and she'd hesitated. His name alone brought back everything she'd experienced the day Gerald was returned from Argentina, how shocked she'd felt meeting him then, his face and clothes still bloodied from his captivity. Seeing him again in London had been upsetting, and she often vaguely wondered since what had happened to him. Would seeing his work possibly again open old wounds long since healed? But, she'd thought, "You can never bury the past. Like it or not, it's part of you. Trying to hide it can only make moving forward more difficult."

Reaching the museum she took a deep breath and went in to view the exhibit.

—❧❧—

Jake's work left her deeply impressed. One photograph after another of a wide variety of people and places around the world showed a profound sensitivity and rare insight into human frailty. Kelly thought his work more than good and memorable.

She spent time looking at the photographs, and when she finally had covered them all, she went out onto a terrace within MOMA where there was warm autumn sun and where she could have coffee. She found an empty table and ordered a latte and was looking around at the pleasant surroundings dominated by a giant La Chaise statue when with a start she realized that Jake himself was seated with a woman two tables away. She thought, "Of course he would be here. It's his exhibit, after all."

There was no avoiding him because, as though fated, Jake had caught sight of her at the same time. With an expression of pleased surprise he came over. "Kelly, I can't believe it." He was wearing a patch over his vacant eye socket and the great scar across his nose and cheek had faded somewhat, and although his clothes were the same as years before, he looked distinguished.

Nothing would do but that she join him and his wife, a warmly pleasant looking woman in her forties, who wore a minimum of jewelry and makeup.

Even before they'd got to his table, with Kelly saying she'd just returned from England and how exciting the exposition of his work was, and Jake telling her that he'd settled down and started his own photographic business, she found herself dreading that he was bound to ask about Gerald.

Getting seated, and before Jake was able to introduce her to the woman who was smiling in welcome, she noticed that the dress sleeve of the woman's left arm was empty, and memory kicked in of the newspapers saying that when kidnapped with Gerald, the arm of the woman, also held captive, had been nearly severed as she'd tried to follow the ransomed Italian to freedom. It couldn't be. But had to be, surely. Even as Jake began to introduce her with "This is my wife," Kelly said to her, "You're Teresa," and, as she did, realized she was smiling herself.

The answer was guileless. "Jake found me two years later. I was working as a hotel bartender in Sydney, Australia." She laughed. "As far from Argentina as I could get."

Time for a moment reeled dizzily back for Kelly. The scandal, the newspaper accounts of the kidnapping, Gerald caught out. And then as fast as memory came with all its depression and anger and futility, it disappeared. This wasn't eight years ago. Jake and this woman, with whom she suddenly felt a common bond, were *now*. She wasn't living as Kelly Anders writing nonsense for romantically starved women and harboring a near dead husband whom she had never sincerely loved. Jake was no longer roving, forever alone and wearily seeking peace, too much in a rut to dare a change. The woman was happily settled in marriage, her dubious past clearly put behind her, and her future secure.

Kelly thought, "To hell with rushing back to my apartment." She put a warm hand on Teresa's. "You know," she said, "this is a kind of an old-school-tie reunion, right? I think we ought to see if they have some champagne some place." She was sure it was what Rachel would have said.

→◆←

Champagne led to dinner and catching up on all that had happened in hers and Jake's different lives, and when she got back downtown, it was quite late. She calmed down Mischief and took the dog for her usual nightly walk along the tree-lined pedestrian and bicycle paths edging the Hudson River, feeling as she went a surprising and unexpected sense of purpose that was almost exuberance.

Still thinking about the evening, she couldn't help but imagine that far off mining camp crammed against the towering Andes, and even while bringing each other up to date, she'd begun to realize that because of all the awful and mindless brutality there, in a place she'd never seen and by people she'd never known, that she shared an unbreakable bond with Jake Barlow: she had experienced equal imprisonment to his being kidnapped when trapped herself by Gerald's resultant vegetative state. Ironically, the cold wind that was Argentina had blown equally on them both.

And then also, during the evening, something quite unexpected had happened. Something in her had unlocked, and she had a sudden, almost blinding understanding that with Jake no longer a victim of the kidnapping, she need not be either. Jake, like her, had shed Argentina and all that had happened there. While still clinging to his nomadic life, he'd found Teresa, and a door to freedom had opened for him. On her part, Kelly now knew, in her book-signing momentary escape from Gerald and all he represented, a door had been opened for her, too, by Rachel. She only had to walk through it the way Jake had.

Coming back to her apartment and sitting alone in the now dreaded living room, she suddenly found herself laughing and crying at once and babbling senselessly until finally she found meaningful words. "No more city, Mischief," she said. "We're free agents now. You'll see."

It was true. She couldn't and wouldn't stay in New York. Then where would she go? She didn't know, but it would be somewhere where she could write in peace. She'd remembered her old illustrator friend. He lived somewhere in the country. Was it Vermont? She couldn't remember. She'd ask his advice.

But what about Gerald? A firmness settled into her. She would not be blamed, or more importantly, blame herself if she was no longer responsible for him; she would transfer his care to his parents. If they couldn't take him in, there'd be a nursing home that would.

And Estella? She remembered quite clearly that her housekeeper and virtual companion still had a family in Nicaragua and had often expressed homesickness and a desire to rejoin them. Some of her last book would finance whatever was Estella's wish.

She located the phone number of her old illustrator friend, and when she finished the call to him, she had arranged to drive up that weekend and locate a place to rent in the small Vermont town where he had settled. She made herself coffee, then, and going to her office wrote a letter to Gerald's parents surrendering him.

She was embarking on a new life. It made a shiver

of excitement run through her. Rachel's notebook was still lying unwrapped on her desk, where she'd put it when she'd arrived back home. She carefully took off the wrapping, and opening the notebook, studied some of Rachel's latest notes for *Bryan's Way*. Then, taking up a pencil, she began to make some notes of her own on a sheet of foolscap.

Dawn, breaking over the city, found her like that. Writing.

ABOUT THE AUTHOR

Born to wealth and privilege in New York, David Osborn chose to spurn both as false icons after World War II combat as a Marine Corps dive bomber pilot. On his own and following brief careers in television and public relations, he expatriated to France when falsely accused of un-Americanism in the infamous Senator McCarthy era, paying his way with a co-authored first motion picture script, *Chase a Crooked Shadow*. When its star-studded success took him from laboring in a rock quarry in France into Britain's film industry, he was launched on a long world-class writing career that saw him dangerously engaged during several Cold War years with Czech anticommunist resistance behind the Iron Curtain. Living in France and England as well as isolated for twelve years in a tiny Alpine village in Switzerland, Osborn authored numerous stellar TV plays and a score of major motion pictures, including *The Trap,*

which earned an Academy Award nomination. Turning novelist with the critical success of *The Glass Tower* followed by the world best-selling classics *Open Season, The French Decision, Love and Treason,* and a half dozen more outstanding thrillers, he has had many imitators, but none reaching the startling originality of his stories, the stunning impact of his flawless page-turning plots, and his literate prose in each that packs a powerful punch with nearly every line.

ALSO BY DAVID OSBORN

Novels and Screenwriting

Novels

The Glass Tower – Hodder & Stoughton

Open Season – The Dial Press

The French Decision – Doubleday

Love and Treason – New American Library

Heads – Bantam

Murder on Martha's Vineyard – Lynx

Murder on the Chesapeake – Simon & Schuster

Murder in the Napa Valley – Simon & Schuster

The Last Pope – Source Books

The Cape Cod Blue – Dagmar Miura

Alicia's Secret (young adult) – Dagmar Miura

A Cold Wind from the Andes – Dagmar Miura

The Head Hunters – Dagmar Miura

Looking Back: The Long Life of a Writer (a memoir)

Delta Red – Dagmar Miura

Eventide – Dagmar Miura

The Somersville Bodies – Dagmar Miura

Cold Case 369 – Dagmar Miura

The Lighthouse (a novella)– Dagmar Miura

The Saugatuck Conspiracy – Dagmar Miura

For Children

Jessica and the Crocodile Knight (a novel)
– HarperCollins

Jessica and Her Adventures in Fairyland (collection of
five novellas) – Dagmar Miura

Ophelia and Her Forest Friends (series of ten stories) –
Dagmar Miura

Jessica and the Witch's Broom – Dagmar Miura

Jessica and the Flying Unicorns – Dagmar Miura

Jessica and the Golden Swan Feather – Dagmar Miura

Feature Films

The Trap (original story and screenplay; Academy Award
nominee for Best Foreign Film) – Columbia

Open Season (screenplay, adapted from Osborn's own
best-selling novel *Open Season*) – Columbia

Chase a Crooked Shadow (original story and screenplay
co-written with Charles Sinclair; listed by the British
Academy of Motion Picture Science as "One of the ten
best suspense scripts ever written") – Warner Bros.

Moment of Danger, a.k.a. *Malaga* (screenplay adapted
from the novel) – Warner Bros.

Malaga (screenplay) – Warner Bros.

Maroc 7 (original story and screenplay) – J. Arthur Rank

Deadlier Than the Male (original story and screenplay) –
J. Arthur Rank

Some Girls Do (original story and screenplay) – J. Arthur
Rank

The Road to Dusty Death (screenplay) – J. Arthur Rank

The Games (screenplay) – Associated British

Follow the Boys (original story and screenplay) – MGM

Beat Girl (original story and screenplay) – Renown Films/ British Lion

Stop-over Forever (original story and screenplay) – British Lion

Winter Holiday (original story and screenplay) – MGM

Penny Gold (original story and screenplay) – J. Arthur Rank/Columbia

Whoever Slew Auntie Roo? (original story and screenplay) – Paramount & American International

Murder, She Said (screenplay, Agatha Christie adaptation) – MGM

Murder at the Gallop (screenplay, Agatha Christie adaptation) – MGM

Feature-Length Documentaries

Fangio, The History of Formula One Racing (original screenplay; executive producer) – Volpi Productions

Why Ireland – Irish Tourist Bureau

Films Canceled While in Production

HMS Ulysses – Volpi Productions (screenplay adaptation of the Alistair MacLean novel about protecting North Sea convoys to Russia during World War II; production halted when a key warship was unavailable)

The Mad Motorists – Volpi Productions (screenplay adaptation from the Allen Andrews novel about the 1907 Peking to Paris race)

Eagle at Sundown – Dragon Films (original screen story about Napoleon's escape from Elba; starring Douglas Fairbanks; in production when canceled)

Les Petits Rats – Disney (original story and screenplay about the Paris Ballet school; production begun, then canceled)

Hunters' Horn – McCahon Productions (screenplay adaptation from the Harriette Simpson Arnow novel; production canceled; financing failure)

Blood on the Rose – British Lion (screenplay adaptation from the Phyllis Hastings novel)

Television

Bouquet for Miss Olive (three-act play; British Television Producers Association nominee for Best Play of the Year) – Granada/ITV

Three on a Gas Ring (three-act play; British Television Producers Association nominee for Best Play of the Year) – Granada/ITV

Why George Brown Hanged (three-act play) – Granada/ITV

Arthur of the Britons (pilot and three scripts on the life of King Arthur; Writers Guild of Great Britain award winner for Best British Children's Series)

The Antiquers (original story, pilot, and six episodes in the sitcom series) – Irish National Television

www.ingramcontent.com/pod-product-compliance
Lightning Source LLC
Chambersburg PA
CBHW010346170726
48284CB00009B/2800